DARK KISS OF

THE REAPER

by

Kristen Painter

PUBLISHED BY:
Kristen Painter

Dark Kiss Of The Reaper
Copyright © 2011 by Kristen Painter
Cover by Kim Killion, Hot Damn Designs

For Elaine,
without whom this
book would not have been.

Chapter One

A slinky sweep of sound pulled Sara's attention from the patient charts in front of her.

What in the...

A man glided down the corridor wearing a silvery robe, which might have been made of chain mail, except the weave looked too fine and moved too fluidly. Satiny gray wings sprouted from his back, their tips long enough to skim the floor. She choked at the sight, nearly spewing her coffee across the charts.

She blinked, but the guy was real, not a trick of the dimmed lighting and long hours. Her hands tightened on the paperwork. Only tonight's full moon could explain the tall, dark madman strolling down the hall dressed like the angel of death.

If he thought for one minute wearing a get-up like that in the cancer ward was funny, he was one twisted individual. Or maybe she was just particularly cranky. She hadn't spent a lot of time in her happy place lately. Ray's being two months behind on alimony payments had a way of doing that. Her lawyer hadn't been much help either. Men. Now she had the freak of the week stalking the ward well after visiting hours. These kind of moments inspired thoughts of quitting.

A hard breath rushed from between her clenched teeth. Who was she kidding? She had no life beyond her work, few friends that she hadn't met at the hospital or at Grounded, the coffee shop where she worked morning shifts. After the divorce, she'd had to move to find an affordable place and the friends she and Ray had shared hadn't made any real attempt to keep in touch with her.

The winged reaper disappeared around the corner. Who dressed like that for a visit to the oncology floor? She'd seen a lot of odd things in her time at Franklin General, but this might win the award for most tasteless. Granted, he wasn't carrying a big, shiny scythe or wearing black, but still. Whatever happened to singing telegrams and guys in gorilla suits delivering balloons? Now those brought a smile to most patients' faces, but this? Whoever had sent Joe Black to deliver their message was one warped individual. Probably good friends with her ex-husband.

She left her coffee and files at the undermanned nurse's station and went after him. Being unit secretary made her especially protective of this floor.

"Sir."

No response. Typical male. Only heard what they wanted to. She fisted her hands. Raising her voice at this late hour would be unkind to the patients who'd been able to fall asleep. She picked up her pace, hoping proximity would substitute for volume.

"Sir, visiting hours are over." Her whisper came out a loud hiss.

He kept moving, his stride purposeful and determined, yet smooth...almost like he was gliding. Weird. She couldn't see how his wings attached, but the way they arched over his broad shoulders and down his back looked pretty sturdy. The costume must have cost a fortune.

Holy crap! She stopped short. Did the wings just move? They must be mechanized. Now several steps behind, she raised her voice as loud as she dared. "Sir!"

No response. Her temper rose a notch.

He opened the door to Edna Metzger's room and slipped inside so deftly that he barely broke his stride. Edna was in the last stages of gastric cancer, but the octogenarian steel magnolia showed little evidence of the pain she suffered. Sara reached for the handle and entered the room as quietly as possible.

The costumed man bent over Edna's bed, his back to Sara. This close, he was even bigger than he'd originally seemed – taller, broader, more ex-linebacker than grown-up cherub. His robes, no longer swirling about him, now outlined wide shoulders and sculpted arms. She glanced at Edna. Thankfully, still sleeping.

Linebacker or angelic whack job, he had to go. Poor Edna. Her one and only visitor was about to get kicked out.

Sara cleared her throat softly. "Sir, you can't be in here. This woman is very ill. She doesn't need to be disturbed. And your outfit is in very bad taste, if you ask me."

He straightened and looked over his shoulder. Smoky eyes circled with chrome glittered beneath straight, dark brows. "You can see me?" His voice slipped across her skin like a warm breath.

Her hands relaxed. Wow...those eyes...had to be contacts. A sweeping calm settled around her like a warm blanket. She blinked, shook her head, refocused.

"The seven-foot wings make you hard to miss."

He turned, his robes opening slightly to reveal a flash of silver near his waist, but before she could identify the object, the robe settled over it. His eyes narrowed. He

8

opened his mouth to speak then closed it, shaking his head as if puzzled.

Seen full on, he was quite a sight. With his chiseled jaw and divinely bowed mouth, he played the part of an angel well. Maybe he was a struggling actor or a wannabe model working an odd job to make ends meet. Although with a face like that, she couldn't see him struggling long. He could be a stand-in for Michelangelo's David. She cleared her throat softly. Now was not the time to be thinking about any man naked, winged or otherwise.

The odd sooty hue of his thick curls must be a wig, or maybe powder in his hair, but his hair looked too soft to be artificial and shone too much to be powdered.

He reached out and touched her shoulder, his fingertips grazing the seam of her sweater.

The slight touch set every nerve in her body on alert. She jerked back. This might be the first contact she'd had with a man in months, but her body shouldn't respond so quickly. It wasn't like she was desperate. Much.

Dropping his hand, he tilted his head. His mysterious eyes tapered with curiosity. "You are alive."

Cute but cracked, and apparently, more gifted with pretty than smart. Tragic, really. Such a waste of great packaging. "Okay, I don't know who you think you are but—"

He took a step closer. A warm, male scent drifted around her, fogging her head. "You can see me, acknowledge my appearance, and yet you don't know who I am or what my purpose is?"

The voice was pure music. And he smelled good enough to lick. But he was still a nut case. She stepped back. "I know you don't belong here. Look, I'm sure you're a nice guy, just doing your job, but you need to leave now or I'm calling security."

"I am Azrael, the Angel of Death."

She rolled her eyes. "Yeah, and the third Tuesday of every month I'm Wonder Woman." She jerked her thumb toward the door. "Let's go. Out. Before you wake Edna and scare the life out of her."

His sly smile knocked her back a step. "As you wish, Sara Donovan." He held up his index finger. "I will give you one night." He nodded in a way she could only call respectful, then brushed past her on his way out the door, swirling more of that delicious maleness around her.

For a moment, she stood motionless. She glanced down at her hospital ID. Of course, her ID. Satisfied that's how he'd known her name, she scanned Edna's sleeping form. Everything seemed in order, but Sara didn't really know what she should be looking for.

Had he taken anything? Left anything behind? What was his purpose? To help the old woman in some way?

His Angel of Death outfit didn't exactly say, "get well soon" but his eyes hadn't been the eyes of a man intent on harm. In fact, there'd been something comforting about his dark gaze. Not to mention sexy.

Couldn't she be attracted to an accountant for once in her life? An accountant would understand the consequences of unpaid alimony. Rolling her shoulders, she blamed the unexplainable attraction on lack of sleep and excessive amounts of caffeine. She shook her head. That was the only reason she could be wondering if Mr. Crazy was free for dinner.

Satisfied all was well with Edna, Sara yawned and checked her watch on her way out of the room. She ought to report the incident to security, but her day had been too long already. She'd make sure the unwanted visitor was gone, then she was going home.

Working full shifts at two different jobs back to back had a way of leaving a body dead tired.

* * *

Sara's alarm clock showed no mercy, yanking her from a particularly vivid dream and shoving her into the cold reality of morning. She snaked one arm from beneath the covers and whacked the offending object until it shut up.

She rolled over and stared at the ceiling, trying to catch the remnants of her dream. White sand, blue water, warm sun, swaying palms...the dream had been the same these last few nights. Except...she blinked...hadn't there been a new element last night? A man on the beach. With wings.

She didn't want to think about what her subconscious was trying to say. At least she'd slept, something that hadn't been coming easily the last few days.

Sighing, she pushed back the quilt and hoisted herself to the edge of the bed, the dream's peaceful feeling ebbing like a midnight tide. A real vacation would be wonderful, but she wasn't going anywhere further than the town square on her budget. Besides, the oncology floor might actually shut down if she left.

Well, maybe it wouldn't shut down, but there would be mass confusion. She smirked. Chaos. Unparalleled disorder. They needed her.

She glanced at the clock, then stuck her tongue out at it. Time to move, whether she wanted to or not.

Her head protested the sudden rise, but she kept motoring toward the kitchen and the coffee that would be waiting. Thank the heavens above for the auto brew feature. She added sweetener, a splash of skim milk, then filled the mug with black gold. She popped two aspirin and gulped them down. The hot coffee went down like a single ray of sunshine on a rainy day. Nice, but not enough. She'd have a double espresso at work, before she started her morning shift at Grounded.

She leaned against the counter, giving herself a few more minutes to wake up and the caffeine time to kick in. The far edge of the laminate needed gluing down again. How did that happen when she never cooked in this kitchen? Not much point in slaving over a gourmet meal for one, and heating up take-out in the microwave and baking frozen pizzas didn't really count as cooking.

Maybe she should get a cat. Something soft and warm to come home to. Of course, if she couldn't keep houseplants alive, what made her think a mammal would be any different?

She rubbed a tender temple with her free hand and exhaled. Another day, another aching head. The headaches were a product of her over-dependency on caffeine, but such was life. Working part-time at a coffee shop was bound to have its drawbacks.

She finished her first cup, went back to the bedroom to change into her running clothes, and hit the street. She loved nothing more about her morning run than getting it over with. The adrenalin boost was an added bonus and helped kick out the pain in her head.

The slap of her sneakers on the dewy sidewalk faded into thoughts of last night's odd visitor, her Caribbean dream, clothes for the day, her two work schedules for the week, which bill needed to be paid, which bill could wait. She turned back into the apartment complex's parking lot with a mental to-do list.

After a quick shower, she dressed, grabbed a change of clothes for her hospital job and headed for Grounded. Already, her body craved another hot cup of caffeinated goodness. On her way in, she left another message for her attorney to get on Ray's case about the alimony he owed.

At the end of her morning shift at Grounded, she went straight to the hospital, changed in the locker rooms and dove into work. The hours went by without incident, a blur of paperwork and tasks completed. The night shift would come on soon, visiting hours would end and a few hours after that, she could head home. In truth, the later it got, the more she liked the hospital. It was quiet at night, the dimmed lighting making it almost peaceful. Or as peaceful as a hospital could be. The emergency room was a different story, but her work rarely took her there.

She approached the nurses' station, her rubber-soled shoes making little noise. The night nurses were a dedicated bunch, and she respected them more than she could say.

She smiled at the familiar dark head bent down in concentration. "Hey you. How's your evening going?"

Manda, the senior staff nurse, looked up from a patient's chart and returned Sara's smile. "Hey girl. Quiet as can be expected." She checked her watch. "You off already? Seems early."

Sara wrinkled her brow. "Early is a relative term. I'm off in a few, then home and..." She sighed. "Sleep and I used to be so well acquainted. Now, not so much." She shrugged.

Manda shook her head, her dark ponytail swinging. "Honey, try working my hours sometime. Sleeping when the sun's shining is wrong on so many levels, but you get used to it after a while." She winked, grinning in a way that spoke volumes about her dedication to her job and where her heart truly lay.

"You're a better woman than I am." Every time Sara thought her two-job schedule was rough, she thought of Manda. Graveyard was a killer, especially when you had a family.

The nurse stood and headed for the office. "See you 'round, girl." She wiggled her ample hips and tapped an imaginary cigarette. "Tell Mr. Sandman I said come up and see me some time."

Sara laughed. "Will do." She waved and walked away. A dark form moved past the corner of her vision as she turned the bend in the hall. She whipped around. Nothing. She rubbed her eyes. It was nothing, wasn't it? Probably. Maybe. Maybe not.

She backtracked to the nurses' station. Manda was still in the office, going through files.

She looked down the right hall, but it was empty. She checked the left. Edna Metzger's door was silently swinging closed. She marched down the hall toward the old woman's room. If that nut job had returned, she was definitely calling security this time. Her hand stopped the door just before it clicked shut. She pushed it open.

Mr. Angel of Death was back.

"That's enough." She reached forward, brushing against one surprisingly warm wing, and grabbed his arm. Corded muscle bunched beneath her fingers. She tried to spin him around, but he was solid and hard to budge. "I told you yesterday, you can't be in here."

Again, those soot-hued eyes peered into hers a little too deeply. "I gave you one night, Sara Donovan. That was all. Now, I must do my work."

Sara grimaced. "Your work?" How much were they paying this guy? "Look, I don't think you get it, but visiting a terminally ill woman dressed like that doesn't fly here. Or in any hospital, I would imagine. You need to leave." She picked up Edna's bedside phone and dialed security. "I need somebody up here now."

"What I do is for the best." He turned back to Edna and embraced her, drawing the elderly woman against his chest. Her eyes fluttered open briefly, a soft smile lit her face, then her body went limp in his arms. He eased her back onto her pillow. The monitors in the room flat-lined.

Sara's jaw slacked. "What did you do?" She dropped the phone. "What *did* you *do*?"

He tipped his head in her direction, staring at her harder than he'd done before. "I told you who I am and what I am here for."

"What you are is a..." She wanted to say psychopath, but telling a nut job he was nuts rarely ended well. A bead of sweat iced her spine. She searched her brain for one single move from the self-defense class she'd taken last spring. He probably outweighed her by a hundred pounds, but she might be able to delay him long enough for security to get here.

He turned, the full width of him blocking her view of anything else. "I am Azrael, the Angel of Death. What you mortals call a grim reaper." His brows angled down, adding to the increasingly ticked off look on his face.

"I'm sure that'll go over big in lock down." Her heart pounded against her rib cage. She fisted her hands and lifted them in front of her, aware of how absurd a move it was. What was she going to do? Box the guy into submission?

He shifted, causing the side of his robe to slip back and reveal a small silver scythe dangling from his belt. The edge gleamed even in the room's dim lighting.

Her blood chilled. Who ever he was, he had definitely done something bad to Edna and now she knew he had a weapon.

She glanced at the old woman's lifeless body then back at him. "You killed her," she whispered, a mix of anger and fear edging her words. "You're not going to get away with that."

He sighed and moved toward the foot of the bed, putting a little more space between them. "The cancer killed her. Or would have in time. I simply reaped her soul before the pain made her life more unbearable than she deserved. Her death was merciful, painless." He glanced at Edna. "As it should be."

Reaped her soul? Sara mentally raised his crazy alert level to orange and stepped back, keeping her hands up. Foolish or not, the stance gave her a sense of protection.

The door swung open and knocked her forward as the requested security guard barreled in. She hit the IV rack, sending it crashing into the wall, and landed on all fours beside the bed. Her knees stung from the impact of the hard linoleum floor. She cursed softly under her breath.

"I'm sorry, Ms. Donovan. You all right? I didn't know you were in front of the door." Oren, the guard, bent to help her.

Over 6'3", he outsized her by almost a foot, but he'd make a good match for the guy with wings.

He lifted her to her feet. "What's going on in here? You okay?"

"I'm fine." Somehow she'd sliced open the side of her hand. She held it up so the blood would run down her arm instead of onto the floor.

"We need the police. I think this guy just killed Mrs. Metzger."

Oren looked over her shoulder, then back at her. "What guy?"

Chapter Two

Sara swung around. The wacko was gone. Gone. How on earth... "There was a guy in here, dressed like an angel. He must have run out when you came in."

Oren shrugged. "I didn't see any—"

"He must be in the hall." She rushed past him and looked in both directions. Oren followed her out. Nothing. Where had he gone so quickly?

Oren put his hands on his hips and looked at her like her brain was on vacation. "I think I would have noticed a guy in an angel suit."

Sara scowled. She was not the crazy he needed to be concerned about. "Call the police. Edna Metzger is dead and I don't think her cancer is the reason why."

He nodded without commitment. "Yeah, you better get that hand looked at."

"I'm serious. Check the halls," she commanded and ran for the nurses' station. "Manda, you see anybody come by here?"

"I thought you went home?" Her eyes widened at the blood dripping down Sara's arm and staining the cuff of her white blouse. "What did you do to yourself?"

"Did anyone run by here? A guy in an angel costume?" She grabbed a few take-out napkins from the desk behind the counter and pressed them to the gash on her hand. He had to be here somewhere. Would he take the elevator or the stairs?

Manda raised her brows. "Honey, what've you been putting in your coffee? Oren came by, but he said he'd been called. You feeling all right?"

"I'm fine," she answered as Oren loped up behind her.

He leaned against the desk, his chest rising and falling with exertion. "Looked everywhere. I can't find anybody, Ms. Donovan. You sure there was a man in that room?"

"Positive. He was wearing a robe and he had wings and some sort of curved blade strapped to his belt."

Oren pursed his lips and shot Manda a look. Manda clucked her tongue like a mother hen and came out from behind the desk. "You sure she didn't hit her head?" she asked Oren as she put her arm around Sara. Manda led her to a nearby wheelchair and pushed her onto the seat. "I'm going to fix up your hand, get a doctor to check you

21

over, maybe give you a little something to calm you down. It's going to be all right, you'll see. Poor child."

Sara struggled a little against Manda's hold on her forearms, but the woman had too much leverage and too much experience dealing with uncooperative patients.

She slumped into the chair and gave up. "You don't understand, he killed her somehow with his grim reaper powers. I'm sure of it."

Manda looked over her shoulder at Oren. "Seriously, she didn't hit her head on anything?"

"Not that I saw."

Manda sighed. "Edna dead?"

"Looks that way."

"Let me take care of her," Manda pointed her chin in Sara's direction, "then I'll get the paperwork started. Find one of the other nurses to go in and confirm, would you?"

Oren nodded. "You got it, Manda. Feel better, Ms. Donovan." He headed down the hall.

"I feel fine," Sara huffed.

Manda shook her head and stared at Sara, her chocolate eyes full of concern and motherly compassion. "Girl, you're going to wear yourself out working these hours. You need a day off, you hear me? This place isn't going to burn to the ground just 'cause you don't show up one day, and that coffee shop can spare you for a day."

"Manda, you don't understand—"

"I do understand. You've got bills to pay. Plus, you've given a lot of your time and effort to this place and you feel like it needs you. Well, you know what? It doesn't need you to be making yourself sick. I know you're stressed about this mess with Ray, too." She sighed and shook her head. "How many sick days you got built up, honey?"

Sara studied the gold cross hanging above Manda's ample cleavage. "Some."

Manda snorted. "Some must mean like a month or two. You take tomorrow off, you understand?"

"I can't, I have—"

"You take tomorrow off from both jobs or I'm going to take you to the psych ward, you dig?"

Sara frowned. "You're a bully, you know that?"

Manda laughed. "Where I come from it's called tough love. Besides, someone's got to mother you since you don't have enough sense to take care of yourself." She released Sara's hands but took hold of her wrist. "Now, let's get that cut looked after."

* * *

Clouds drifted past the estate's expansive limestone balcony. Flowering vines wrapped its banisters and spilled perfume into the air. Carved columns flanked the house's arched doorways, but curtains of milky gauze blurred the rooms beyond. The sound of running water

23

lilted from an unseen fountain. Meant to soothe, Azrael supposed. It wasn't working today.

His jaw tightened.

"Why does she see me? How is this possible?" He knew his tone carried more edge than the Fates had ever heard from him. So be it. They owed him an explanation.

Klotho, the Virgin, set her distaff down and looked up from her golden spindle. The most beautiful of the three, the ever-youthful blonde spun the thread of life. Her shapely brows rose above her sparkling blue eyes, her delicate mouth curving in a subtle smile. "Perhaps she's a Shade."

Normally, facing such beauty made his mind wander. Today, agitation kept his thoughts sharply focused. He closed his eyes for a moment and pictured Sara. "She's flesh and blood, I assure you."

"And you know this because?" Lachesis, the Mother, kept her eyes on her work, measuring life threads against her silver rod. He could barely see her profile through the faded Titian curls surrounding her mature face. From the inflection of her voice, he knew her sea green eyes crinkled with mirth.

"She touched me." Heat flooded him at the memory. Unlike his brothers Kol and Chronos, he had kept himself from the lure of mortal flesh. Sara's touch had aroused an

24

instant desire to lose that control. He could not allow it again. He would not become like his brothers.

Bellowing from inside, Atropos' cackle stirred his displeasure. The Crone was the least sympathetic of the Fates, and rightly so, as she was also the one who chose which threads to sever. Although the Reapers loathed admitting it, she was their boss. Azrael ground his teeth thinking about it. Atropos wielded power enough in her shears. Someday, he would find Nyx, mother of the Fates, and speak to her about her daughters. Or at least one of them.

Atropos pushed through the gauzy curtains, allowing a brief glimpse into the home's interior. Her carved-bone cane clicked against the creamy marble tiles of the balcony. "Touched a mortal, did you?"

"She touched me, but it was nothing." Nothing but a single moment of contact he couldn't stop reliving. Sara Donovan was so warm. So alive.

Atropos settled into a gilded chair beside Klotho. A silver-streaked braid draped one hunched shoulder and more wisps of gray hung about her weathered face. The fatal shears, forged of lightning and etched in runes, hung in their pouch at her waist.

"Falsehoods do not become you, Reaper." She shrugged. "But that is not my concern. Nor do I understand why you deny yourself human contact. Wipe the memory and they know nothing."

"I will not abuse my power." What Chronos and Kol did was their own business. He was the Reaper of Mercy. To him, that demanded a certain conduct.

Again, she shrugged. "I'm too tired to argue your unnecessary sense of morality."

He clenched his fists to keep from reacting and took a deep breath. Atropos had a way of igniting his temper that none other did. He'd spent enough time here. He wanted an answer. "What of the mortal woman?"

Her knobby fingers griped the chair's gryphon-headed arms as she leaned forward. "What matters is not how she sees you or why, but rather that she does."

He scowled. Doddering old manipulator. Always speaking in rhymes and riddles. She was one of the Fates, not the Oracle of Delphi. "What in Hades is that supposed to mean?"

"Temper, temper." She smiled, revealing yellow teeth. "Perhaps you should talk less and think more. What you want and what you need are two different things."

He looked at the other two women, wondering if they had anything to add. Klotho hummed softly to herself. Lachesis shook her head as though she pitied him. If that was true, she wasted her sympathy.

Unfurling his wings and letting the Darkness fill his eyes, he leaned forward and stared Atropos down. "I am Death. And Death needs nothing."

Back in his own domain, Azrael paced the thick rug covering the floor of his great hall while Vitus, the Shade that served as his butler, ushered in Azrael's brothers. The life the Fates had granted Vitus in order to serve Azrael had not included a voice, so the man raised his brows, the question of whether or not Azrael needed anything else in his eyes.

"That is all, thank you." Azrael paused long enough to dismiss Vitus. The man nodded and Azrael returned to his pacing. The wool beneath his feet absorbed the sounds of his footfalls, but not the mutterings of his brother, Kol, the deadliest kind of reaper, a Thresher.

"Why am I here?" Kol's dark glasses hid his deadly eyes but not the aggravated set of his jaw.

Azrael's other brother, Chronos, the Timekeeper, rolled his eyes. He sat in a nearby tapestry chaise, stretched his long legs out and tipped his head to stare at Kol. "You are not the only one who's been called."

Kol snorted, but held his tongue. He draped one leather-clad arm over the vast marble mantel surrounding the walk-in fireplace, tipped his head against the wall, and stared at the sky mural painted on the ceiling.

27

Chronos turned back to Azrael. "Why have you called us, brother?"

Azrael blew out a breath and stopped pacing. He glanced once at both Chronos and Kol, then focused on the carpet. Calling upon his brothers was a rare event. Especially Kol. "The Fates have...been meddling in my life."

Kol's sharp laugh split the air. "Finally sunk their hooks into you, huh? Welcome to the club."

"In what way?" Chronos asked, ignoring Kol.

Azrael arrowed a look at Kol. He shrugged and Azrael continued. "They have caused a mortal to see me. One who isn't appointed to me."

Chronos wrinkled his brow. "We can all be seen in our mortal forms."

Kol cursed. He had a human form, but it was the same as his reaper form. He was no more approachable in either appearance. For that, Azrael could forgive Kol's displeasure. Not having a true mortal form must make life very hard indeed.

"I wasn't in my mortal body. What's worse is she's even seen me reap a soul."

Kol's cursing died away. "Seriously? Why would they allow that?"

Chronos stood, shaking his head. A tear opened along the shoulder of his ever-aging black robe. A swarm of tiny metallic spiders streamed from beneath the fabric, repaired the rip and disappeared again. "There must be a reason. The Fates have their ways, even if we do not understand them."

"Mumbo jumbo," Kol spat, pushing off the mantel and coming closer. "If this woman can see you as a Reaper, it can only come to a bad end."

Chronos slanted his eyes at Kol. "Is that what happens to the women you keep company with?"

He responded with ice in his voice. "The women who entertain me don't understand who I am."

"Neither do we," Chronos muttered.

Azrael held his hands up. "I called you here for help, not to pit you against one another."

Kol pulled off his dark glasses, revealing eyes like burning embers, eyes capable of sucking in human souls with a glance. "You want me to take care of her?"

"No!" Azrael cleared his throat. "No." He hadn't meant for the word to come out as a shout. So desperate. So concerned. He rubbed his palm against his temple. The situation worsened by the moment. His brothers weren't offering the help he'd hoped for. He should have known.

Kol smiled and slid his glasses back into place. "I'm beginning to understand."

Chronos shook his head slowly, his grave expression unmistakable. He clasped Azrael's shoulder. "Humans have no permanent place in our world, and we have only a brief place in theirs."

"At least not for more than a night or two." Kol waggled his brows at Chronos.

Idiot. And Chronos was just as bad. Azrael shrugged off his brother's hand. "You're both making assumptions based on your own weaknesses.

Kol's mouth thinned. "I have no weaknesses." He jabbed his finger at Azrael and Chronos. "You want to talk weak? You two live like kings with your servants."

Chronos tossed his head in mock laughter. "Repurposed Shades do not a kingdom make."

Ignoring his brother's comment, Kol focused on Azrael. "You want to trade scythes with me? Walk my path? I don't think so. If I occasionally get some small pleasure with a willing woman it's really none of your concern."

"Agreed." Azrael's ire cooled a bit. He had no desire to take on Kol's desolate life. Vitus and the other servants may not be able to speak, but they were a form of company. Kol had no one.

"I think you should have a dalliance, get this woman out of your system, then leave her alone. Of course, you're free to make your own mistakes." Chronos said.

Kol folded his arms against his chest. "What he said. Stay away from her, or don't, but don't come crying to us when things hit the crapper."

"I don't plan on crying to either of you about anything. And no one tells me what to do or how to conduct myself. Am I clear? Now, get out. Both of you." Azrael turned toward the windows overlooking his perpetually twilight world. Why he'd thought his brothers would offer some help or insight, he didn't know. As always, they were useless, treating him like a child in need of guidance, not a peer. Inviting them had been a mistake.

He blew out a hard breath, leaned his hand against the window frame. They lived their lives with great abandon and no thought for consequence. They had no place to tell him how to live his.

If he wanted to see Sara Donovan again, no one was going to stop him.

* * *

Not long into her day off, Sara ditched her pajamas and dressed for her shift at the hospital. She may have missed her shift at Grounded, but she could still make the one at Franklin. Her hand was fine. Her head hadn't ached once. She'd gone for a run, done laundry, organized her DVDs alphabetically, drunk a pot and a half of coffee, glued down the loose edge of the counter and cleaned out her fridge. She was afraid if she didn't go in, she'd end up at a pet store or the ASPCA. Then some poor feline would be subject to a life of loneliness and obesity due to guilt-motivated table scraps.

Or worse, she'd drive to Mercy Memorial where Ray worked, find her lowlife ex and get the alimony without her lawyer's help.

The possibility she might accost Ray wasn't the only reason, though. Getting out of the house and getting busy might help her stop thinking about *him*.

The Angel of Death guy.

At work, she'd be too occupied for her mind to wander in his dark, sexy direction. She shouldn't want to think about him at all considering he might have killed Mrs. Metzger. Although, in his defense, she'd called the hospital to check and found they'd written the death off as cancer-related. There'd be no autopsy. She sighed as she zipped the back of her skirt. Maybe it *was* the cancer after all. What could he have possibly done to her without leaving a mark and in such a short amount of time? Hugging someone had yet to be fatal.

So what did it mean that she couldn't stop thinking about a guy this odd? She pushed her hair out of her face, pulling it back into a loose ponytail before adding small silver hoop earrings. Women fell for weirdoes all the time. Some of them even married guys on death row. Not that she thought she'd hit that level of desperation yet.

Besides, this guy hadn't actually been convicted of killing anyone. That she knew of.

She searched for another reason her brain kept replaying images of him while she slicked cranberry gloss across her lips. He *was* handsome. But lots of guys were good looking. Maybe not that good looking, but whatever.

Grabbing her purse off the small table by the door, she focused on what needed doing at the hospital. A few hours later, she was buried in paperwork and charts. When Manda arrived, she gave Sara the expected grief about showing up on what was supposed to be a day off.

"I was going a little crazy. It was come to work or buy a cat. I came to work."

"That's no excuse. Cat might be good for you."

"Yes, but I might not be good for the cat. Plus I feel fine."

"Have you seen anything unusual around here today?"

"No." Sara gave her a smirk. No point discussing the reaper with Manda. The woman would drag her off to the psych ward, no questions asked. Manda always made good on her threats.

By the end of the week, Sara had managed three shifts in a row without a single sighting of the lone reaper.

Tonight would make four. She stretched at the desk, rolling her shoulders. She was adult enough to admit he might have been a hallucination. A tangible one, but heaven knew with the hours she worked and the general craziness of her life it was certainly a possibility.

Her stomach rumbled. Maybe instead of take-out for dinner tonight, she'd make pasta. Real honest-to-goodness home cooking. She laughed. Yeah, honest-to-goodness out of a box and jar, but hey, it was a place to start.

Head lost in thoughts of garlic bread and fettuccine Alfredo, she recalculated the figures laying on the desk in front of her for the second time, stabbing the numbers on her calculator with a pencil eraser. Still not right. She added them a third time. Crap. Some of the hours on the nurses' schedule Manda had put together weren't adding up right.

She checked her watch. Half an hour before Manda came on and could straighten this mess out. Sara logged onto the computer and worked another project to wait for the night shift to arrive.

Through the hall windows, the sky purpled behind clouds that hid the full moon. The hospital had already quieted down as visiting hours were over. In another hour, the corridor lights would dim. The hum of machines, usually unheard during the bustling day, would vibrate in the background like a chorus of mechanical crickets. A lot of people didn't like hospitals. Didn't like what went on in them. But to Sara, there was a safety here like nowhere else. Yes, bad things happened within these walls. But there were two sides to every coin.

Life breathed its first breath here, made its first cry. Lives were saved, people healed. And sometimes...sometimes death came as a relief to those who suffered, both patient and family alike.

There was nothing to fear within these walls.

Nothing at all.

Chapter Three

Since Manda needed to go through patient charts before she'd have time to go over the schedules, Sara headed to the visitor's room to coax a bottle of water from the ancient vending machine. The room was dark, but she didn't flip the switch. Between the machine's soft glow and the residual light from the hall spilling in there was plenty to see by.

She dug in her cardigan pocket for the dollar bills kept for just this purpose. Nothing. She checked the other pocket and sighed. Time to refill the singles.

Empty-handed, she turned and thudded into something hard.

And warm.

And so not a hallucination.

"Sara Donovan."

The voice skittered through her with familiar heat. She knew it, before she even looked up. "You..." Backing away, she lifted a finger to point. Her hand trembled.

"Azrael," he said, as though she'd forgotten.

"I know who you are." A frightening thought shuffled her back another step. She bumped into the vending machine and swallowed, wondering if something bad was about to happen to her. "Why did you come back? Are you here for me?"

He nodded, a slight smile softening his beautiful mouth. "I had to come back. You can see me."

A little shiver ripped down her spine. So that was it. She'd seen what he'd done to Edna – whatever that was – and now he was here to make sure she kept her mouth shut.

"If you try anything, so help me, I'll scream loud enough to wake the dead." She raised her hands as she had the night in Edna's room, this time flattening them like blades. "I know karate. I can kill a man twelve different ways without breaking a sweat." Complete and utter lie, but considering the circumstances, very forgivable.

The smile thinned. "I am not here to harm you." Something dark flickered in his eyes. "Only to understand more about you."

"You don't need to understand anything about me except that I'm going to start counting, and if you're not gone by the time I hit three, the screaming begins."

"Scream all you want. Anyone who comes to your aid will find you in an empty room."

"You can't run that fast." Or maybe he could. He'd disappeared into thin air the last night she'd seen him.

"I don't intend to run anywhere." He crossed his arms over his chest and stared at her with such intensity her head swam.

Her hands dropped a half-centimeter. "What do you mean?" But she already had a feeling.

"No one sees me but you."

Crap. That was the feeling she'd had. "That's crazy. Or it means I'm crazy. And I'm not." She swallowed, exhaled hard. Her hands fell a little lower.

"You're not crazy. But you are special."

She groaned softly. A guy who thought he was death personified also thought she was special. Was there anything that said loser more than that? "I think you might be the crazy one. Actually, I know you are."

A tinny squeak accompanied the door opening. Manda stuck her head in. "Your head hurting you again?"

"No, not exactly..." Didn't Manda see him?

"Then why you hanging out in the dark?"

Sara looked past the silky curve of one wing. Nothing about Manda's expression indicated she saw anything unusual. "No reason. Do you...see anything...odd about this room?"

"Other than my unit secretary looking like she's about to karate chop someone, no." Manda's pursed lips did little to hide the laughter in her eyes.

Sara dropped her hands. "I'll be there in a minute. I was just getting some water."

"Sure you were." Manda snorted. "See you later, Bruce Lee." She closed the door, humming *Everybody Was Kung Fu Fighting* as she went.

Holy crap on an invisible biscuit. Manda hadn't seen him. "She didn't see you."

Looking rather vindicated, he smirked. "As I said, it's only you."

She rubbed her forehead. "I'm seeing ghosts. I've lost my mind and I'm seeing ghosts."

He laughed softly, putting music in the air. "I'm not a ghost, I am the Angel of Death."

She stared at him from beneath her lashes. "And that's different how?" She shook her head. Having a headache was better than this. "I don't believe you, you know. I think you're insane and you need help. Which is unfortunate because a guy that looks like you really, really ought to be sane."

A single dark brow lifted to punctuate his stony face. "Shall I prove it to you?"

"What? That you're not crazy?"

"That I am the Angel of Death."

New fear flooded her mind in a cold rush. Was that a threat? "What do you mean? What are you going to do?"

He held out his hand. "Take you with me."

"What? No way. Where?" She shook her head. His hand stretched out before her, tempting her to reach for him. Thick, uncalloused fingers and a broad, lined palm. Half of her thought going with a man this gorgeous couldn't be a bad thing – why not call his bluff? – and the other half thought her first half needed to be institutionalized.

"Don't touch me. I'm not going anywhere with you. You're not even really here." That had to be it. She was hallucinating. Why, she had no idea, but it was better than believing a real live grim reaper was trying to abduct her.

"Sara."

He whispered her name so softly she wasn't sure she'd heard it at all. She looked into his eyes and the edges of her peripheral vision blurred away. Such a kind face. Such a comforting smile...

His hand tightened over hers. She startled, unaware she'd put her hand in his until the feel of his warm grasp woke her from whatever fugue state she'd slipped into. She'd been right about no calluses, but his skin held a pleasant roughness—what was she doing? She yanked her hand back, surprised when he let it go without a fight. "This is crazy."

"Sara." Again, that same soft, sexy whisper. "How else will you know the truth?"

"There's got to be another way."

"No harm will come to you, I swear it." He extended his hand.

Trust me. The words sighed through her. She nodded, unable to squelch the trepidation in her belly, but also unable to deny the magnetic pull to discover more about this man.

The edges of her vision blurred further, obscuring what was real and what wasn't. He led her into the hall, or what used to be the hall.

Her heart skidded against her ribs. Fog spiraled around the pale flanks of an enormous horse. It shook its great head, tossing a cloud-colored mane and snorting hot breath. She jumped behind Azrael. His wing brushed her cheek, soft as kitten fur. Better a crazy man than a flesh-eating horse from hell.

"What the crap is that?" She stared at the creature. *Deep breath, deep breath, this is probably just a dream.* She'd rather have the Caribbean back. That didn't scare the pee out of her. She inhaled his warm, male scent, like vanilla pipe smoke and leather.

"That's Pallidus, my horse." He reached out and rubbed the beast's snowy neck. "Nothing to be afraid of."

Azrael slipped his arm around her waist and drew her out from behind him. The intimate touch melted her knees. She grabbed hold of his bicep for support, her fingers barely spanning the muscle.

"Pallidus knows you are to be protected."

"He does? How do you know? What are you, the horse whisperer of grim reapers?" She tried to back away, but Azrael's arm didn't budge. "He looks...hungry."

Azrael gave a short laugh, softening the edge of her nerves. "He hasn't eaten anyone yet."

"It's the yet that worries me."

"He's very partial to having his nose rubbed."

She inched her hand toward the animal. His gray eyes focused on her. He dipped his head. Swallowing, she let her fingers brush Pallidus' nose. Warm and velvety. It seemed impossible that a creature with a nose like a baby's bottom could mean her any harm. She gave him a little scratch and let out the breath she'd been holding.

"Okay, you have a horse. That doesn't prove you're the Angel of Death." How he'd gotten the animal in the hospital, she had no idea. Manda would have a freakin' fit if this animal dropped its business on her floor.

"We've only begun." Azrael mounted the horse in one fluid movement, then held his hands out to her. "Come."

"You've got to be kidding. I'm not getting on that thing."

Pallidus snorted and stomped a hoof.

She held her hands up. "Sorry, you're not a thing. You're a very lovely animal. Really. Can't say when I've seen a more beautiful stallion in my life." Now she was apologizing to a horse. How much further could the weird envelope be pushed?

Pallidus whinnied softly and Azrael laughed and patted the horse's side.

"Are you two...talking?" Apparently, there was tons of room left in that envelope.

He nodded. "In a sense, yes." He held out his hands again.

"No."

"Sara."

What was it about the way he said her name? Reluctantly, she took his hands. He lifted her easily, seating her sidesaddle in front of him.

"Bring your other leg over." He patted Pallidus's other side.

Good thing she'd worn pants today. She did as he asked, settling onto the horse's back. Azrael's muscled thighs cradled hers. His warmth seeped through her trousers, melting her nerves into an acquiescent puddle. She exhaled, hotter than she'd been in a long time. "There aren't any reins. What am I going to hold onto? I don't want to fall off this thin—horse."

"Take hold of Pallidus' mane if need be."

Threading her fingers into the horse's thick white hair, Sara glanced over her shoulder.

"Where exactly are we going?"

And why didn't I ask that before I got on this beast?

* * *

Azrael hesitated. What to tell her that wouldn't frighten her? He realized what she was about to see might scare her more than was healthy, but then again...it might not. And it would undoubtedly prove who he was. "I have work to do. I'm taking you with me."

He slipped an arm around her waist to keep her secure. The move pressed her further against him, connecting them thigh to thigh, bottom to groin, back to chest. The feel of her seduced him with a fierceness that took his breath. He inhaled sharply, drinking in air as he searched for a safe place to focus.

There was none.

He sank into her rich warmth, let it flow around and through him until it possessed him like a dragonfly trapped in amber. The softness of her curves set his hands to trembling. But the scent of her was what threatened to undo him.

Life. The very essence of it perfumed her. Joy and happiness, sorrow and pain, laughter and tears. Vibrant and electric, it buzzed through him, nothing like the faint hum of life left in the mortals whose souls he reaped. This was hot and thick and real. No wonder his brothers craved mortal touch.

Already overwhelmed, he inhaled more of her, his eyes closed against the unbearable wonderfulness sparking through him. When he opened his eyes, he knew it was too late. He was enslaved. Addicted. There would be no turning back. He wanted her.

But more than that...he wanted her to want him in return. There was no other way being with her would be possible.

"Remember," he whispered through her straight brown locks, gathering his control in a tight fist. "Nothing will harm you. I promise."

She leaned into him, tipping her head back to meet his gaze. "I don't know why, but I believe you. I feel safe with you. I don't have a reason to, but I do."

Her lips were so close it would take but a slight bend of his head to match them to his, but her words stopped him. She felt safe. He would not jeopardize that feeling and risk losing whatever small trust had begun to build between them.

"Good." The single word was all he could manage. He nudged Pallidus' sides and the animal moved forward. Mist enveloped them, obscuring Sara's world while they shifted into his.

The mist gave way. Sara gasped, her nails dug into his arm. So that was pain. The sensation intrigued more than it hurt.

A soft cry escaped her and she pressed into him, turning her face into his chest and clutching handfuls of his robe. "Is this real? Tell me this isn't real."

He gazed down onto the earth below. Clouds disappeared beneath Pallidus' hooves as he galloped though the sky.

"It is, but there's no need to be afraid."

"Not from where I'm sitting." She clung tighter.

"It's safe, I promise." Instinctively, he wrapped his arms around her and held her. Zeus Almighty, she felt good in his arms. He was rewarded with the slight relaxing of her tense form.

"Pallidus can fly?" She peered around his shoulder. "Without wings?"

"He doesn't need them. He's a very special horse." How else to explain Pallidus' ability? The horse was bred from the ancient line of Pegasus, but chances were Sara wouldn't believe that either.

She eased up so she could look him in the eyes, but maintained her grip on his robes. "You told me I was special, now you say Pallidus is special – mind you, I'm not disagreeing. You don't get much more special than a flying horse, but being put in the same category as a one is...well...disconcerting."

He bit his tongue to keep from laughing. Instead, he willingly drowned in her beautiful eyes. Copper, bronze, and gold, with shades of cinnamon, coffee and cocoa. He'd never known brown could be so rich or so delicious. One hand slipped up to caress her cheek, just a finger trailed along her jaw, nothing more. He wouldn't risk it.

After this time with him, she would see who he really was. Once she fully understood, she might never want to see him again. Or might not be able to. Who knew what cruel trick the Fates would play next? Either way, he feared Kol's words coming true – that Sara's seeing him could only come to a bad end.

He refused to give place to that thought. He had a job to do, lives to finish with a merciful death. If Sara disappeared from his existence after today, there would be time enough later to deal with it.

Pallidus swept lower toward the earth's surface. Sullen clouds dark with rain and charged with lightning rose past them on their descent. The storm that brewed would claim many lives. The world below focused, the shapes of people and tin-roofed homes became visible. Faint human cries reached his ears. Sara shuddered and he knew she heard them too.

He kept one arm around her, but loosed the other to reach into his robes for his scythe.

"Stay close now. My work begins."

Chapter Four

The ground below swept up toward them with frightening speed. They came in over a churning sea. Deep grooves eroded the beach. Sara clutched Azrael's arm so tightly she knew her grip must be uncomfortable for him, but she didn't care.

Palms flailed in the swirling wind, lashed with sheets of slanted rain. Lightning blinded, glinting off the windows of a few small beachside hotels. And yet, she, Azrael and Pallidus were untouched.

People ran through the streets, their cries for help ringing in her ears. Where were they? Somewhere in the Caribbean, maybe, judging by the coloring of the people and the wording on the signs.

How was this real? As much as she might want to think it was a dream, it wasn't. She was trembling, that was real. The hospital had disappeared. Her world as she'd known it was gone. She was on the back of a flying horse with a man who claimed to be the Angel of Death. And heaven help her, he just might be.

He wasn't entirely human, she accepted that much, but the gentleness with which he touched her, the reassuring strength of his arm around her waist, the spark in his eyes when he looked at her—all those things made her not care.

There was no good reason for it, but she felt safe with him. Feeling that way was crazy, just like everything else that concerned him. And she knew, as much as she knew anything, that no matter who he was, he wouldn't hurt her. She sensed it. He was different, to say the least, but dangerous? She didn't think so.

Azrael reached between them, his hand brushing across her back. A moment later, he stretched his arm out. She tensed. In his hand he held the small silver scythe she'd seen hanging on his belt.

The weapon gleamed with an unnatural light. He held it out from his body and it expanded in his grasp, lengthening and extending. Focusing on anything else but the wicked blade became impossible. He juggled the handle, adjusting his grip.

A whimper reached her ears and she realized it had come from her own lips. He pressed close to her, his breath warming her neck.

"Don't be afraid."

"Easy for you to say." Something dark moved beyond the edges of her vision. She whipped her head around. "What was that?"

He looked in the same direction. "I don't see anything."

Whatever had been there was gone.

"Never mind," she said. Probably a bird or piece of debris in the air. There was enough stuff flying past them to make anyone think they were seeing things.

Pallidus brought them overtop a group of people running down the street. He kept pace with them easily. Azrael leaned off to the side, arching back his great scythe. His robe fell down to his elbow, revealing a forearm corded with muscle. She followed his sight line.

He aimed for the people below.

"What are you doing?" But she already knew. Or thought she did. When he twisted, she reached for his arm. She had to stop him.

"My job, Sara. This is what I do."

"You're going to kill them!"

"Sara, look behind us."

She sat up, turning her head. A huge black storm wall yawned across the beach behind them. It spun like a giant top, swallowing trees, huts, cars, anything in its path.

"Hurricane," she whispered. She met Azrael's patient gaze, tears blurring her vision. "They're going to die anyway, aren't they?"

He nodded.

She closed her eyes hard and took a deep breath. His arm tightened around her waist, a comfort, no matter how small. She pressed her forehead to the side of his neck to further block the sight of the hungry storm.

Azrael stretched taut, and she knew what he was about to do. She opened her eyes, unable to keep herself from watching.

The scythe flashed as it soundlessly sliced the air. It cut through the crowd and to her eyes, looked as though it passed through every person. She raised her head to see over his shoulder, between the calm valley of his wings.

Six peopled crumpled to the ground. The remainder of the group kept running, didn't even slow. That's when she saw the dark object again. It dropped in behind them like a hellish bird of prey, all darkness and smoke. Another horse and rider with nothing but wind beneath them.

Another reaper? She watched, transfixed. The black horse had fire in its eyes and sparks at its hooves. The rider's black leather coat billowed out behind him, cracking the air. She couldn't see his eyes through his dark glasses, but she wasn't sure she wanted to.

Maybe he was some kind of demon. Or not.

He raised a scythe the same size and shape as Azrael's. Except the tarnished blade had a serrated edge caked with either rust or blood. She shivered uncontrollably. The dark reaper reached back, pulling the scythe through the air effortlessly, and brought it down toward the crowd. Azrael shifted, blocking her view.

"There's more than one of you," she mumbled, her stomach churned. She was no longer sure if she was even still breathing. She was glad she hadn't seen the second scythe cut through the crowd. Something told her that blade didn't cut as clean as Azrael's.

Furrowing his brow, Azrael glanced behind. His head snapped back a moment later. His wings unfurled partially, further obstructing her backward view.

"Don't look at him. Look at me or Pallidus or the ground, whatever you have to, but don't look at him."

"Why?"

Before Azrael could answer, the dark reaper pulled along side them. He glanced at her, then Azrael. His mouth curled in a sneer. "You're a fool to bring her. If you want to scare her to death, you should have left her to me."

Azrael pointed his scythe in the other reaper's direction. "Leave her be, Kol."

Kol laughed. The sound reminded Sara of the laughter heard in haunted houses as a child, dark, maniacal and not at all happy. He pulled his glasses down, revealing the blackest eyes she'd ever seen.

The world fell away. Dizziness swept through her as though she stood at the edge of a high cliff about to topple over. Her head swam with vertigo. The wind she hadn't felt before suddenly buffeted her body. Rain stung her face. Her grip on Azrael loosened. She cried out, clutched at him, the sensation of falling too real. Her stomach knotted, unknotted, rolled and dropped. She was going to be sick.

"I have you, you won't fall." Azrael shot out with his scythe, nearly striking the other reaper. Kol moved out of the way, shoved his glasses back into place and urged his horse on. The creature's hooves rent the air with swirls of smoke and thunder.

"He's gone." Azrael's jaw hardened into stone.

Her equilibrium returned. She shuddered. "What...who was that? Another reaper?"

"Yes. In a sense." The word was a growl. "Kol is my brother."

"Your brother?" That Azrael would claim such a being worried her. "He's a..." What could she say? *Your brother's a real jerk? I think he tried to kill me?*

"He wouldn't have hurt you. He was only being Kol. Testing you to see if you could see him as well. It will not happen again. I promise."

"Only being Kol? Testing me? Like that makes it all right?" Anger replaced fear. This whole excursion had just become some sort of bad Tim Burton movie and she was in no mood to become anyone's *Corpse Bride*.

"I'm not making excuses for him. There are none. He is unpleasant at best, but he is who he is."

The wind and rain disappeared. The protective bubble that enclosed Azrael and Pallidus included her once again. Feeling slightly mollified, Sara couldn't help but probe further. "And that might be?"

"Kol is a different kind of Reaper than I am. He's a Thresher. He culls the souls that no longer deserve a mortal existence. Where I reap souls that are ready and deserving of a merciful death, he reaps souls that have misused their time."

Thresher. Thinking about what that meant made her stomach knot again. She swallowed. "I don't like him."

The slightest curve bent Azrael's mouth. "Neither do I, much of the time. But one cannot pick their family, can they?"

She settled against the hard warmth of his chest, letting it relax her. "No, I guess they can't."

"I have more work to do." The statement had a questioning undertone, as if he was asking her how much more she could stand.

"I know." Working in the hospital made death somewhat easier to accept. And she wasn't ready to leave him yet.

"Does that mean you accept who I am?"

"How can I not?" He was really and truly the Angel of Death. Considering everything that had happened in the last few moments that no longer seemed odd. So long as he wasn't her for her, but that was a conversation she wasn't ready to have.

His lips brushed her temple so delicately she wondered if it had actually happened the second after. "You are the right woman, Sara Donovan."

She wanted to ask 'the right woman for what', but she was afraid of the answer. The day had held enough surprises, enough weird answers and bizarre happenings. Why warp it completely by finding out she was supposed to be some sort of human sacrifice or something like that? Right now, she just wanted to breathe and be happy she had the ability to draw the breath.

And yet, there was so much she wanted to understand. How did he know which souls to reap? What determined which souls he took and which he didn't?

Where did the souls go? Had he always been the Angel of Death?

Why could she see him when no one else could?

They continued on in silence, him with his work, her with her observations. The people whose souls he took, she noticed, usually succumbed with a peaceful look on their faces. Kol's victims—for she had come to think of them that way—did not. She couldn't help but watch the other reaper. Thankfully, he ignored her. Even so, she was careful not to make eye contact with him again.

She leaned forward, splaying her hands over Pallidus' muscled shoulders. She needed to feel life, even if it wasn't human.

Azrael moved his arm from about her waist, placing his hand on her hip instead. She turned to look at him, this man—being, creature, whatever he was—who held the power of death in his hands. "I don't know how you do this with such...such...sense of purpose...such calm."

A muscle in his jaw ticked, then smoothed out. His eyes softened with...sadness? Longing? She couldn't tell. He was a hard man to read. "It's all I know."

That she understood. She'd felt that way herself once after a marriage gone bad and a life that seemed to have no purpose. But everything could be changed, couldn't it? Hadn't she proved that with her own life?

"What would you rather do?"

His eyes widened briefly, his lips parted. Then all was stone again. "Nothing," was his answer.

She didn't believe him, but she let it drop. Men, whether they were anesthesiologists or Angels of Death, didn't do emotion well it seemed. Not that she was lumping Azrael in with Ray. She wasn't. Wouldn't.

Her mouth bent in a depreciating frown. Thinking of Azrael as a possibility was proof she'd really lost her mind. He wasn't even human. Shaking her head, she let her chin drop to her chest and half shut her eyes. Being alone was better than being with Ray.

Azrael's hand tensed at her hip. "Are you all right, Sara?"

Touched by the note of concern in his voice, she nodded and blinked. "I'm fine. Just thinking."

He sighed, his breath teasing the back of her neck. "I understand this must be a great deal to comprehend. Perhaps I should not have brought you."

"No, no, not at all. You're right that this is a lot to take in, but I'm glad you chose to share it with me. It's amazing in its own weird way." The ground beneath them faded as Pallidus rose. "I never would have thought something like this possible."

"There would be no way to explain it in words," he said.

"I wouldn't have believed you anyway."

"I'm glad you came." He held the scythe out from his body, spoke a word and the scythe shrank down to its original size. He tucked it back into his robe. "No human has ever seen what we do."

"And lived to tell about it?" She made a joke of it, but the answer hung between them like a hangman's noose waiting to be tightened.

"No." His whispered acknowledgement didn't frighten her. What was to be, would be.

"It's okay," she said. "I'm not afraid."

"Nor should you be. You're in no danger, I swear it." His free hand came to rest on her other hip, tripping sparks over her skin. "You are a most unusual woman."

She tipped her head to look at him. "You're the most interesting man I've met in a long time." She laughed, catching what she'd just said. "You're not really a man, though, are you?"

His grin held a hint of wickedness that spun heat deeper into her bones. "Oh, I am a man, Sara Donovan. Be very sure of that."

Chapter Five

Never had Azrael wanted to harm Kol more than he did now. Sara had come through Kol's "testing" without injury, but that didn't lessen Azrael's need to punish his brother. Somehow, somewhere, Kol would be made to understand his indiscretion.

Azrael moved his head a few inches, burying his nose in her hair, and inhaled. She was perfection. Sweet, opinionated, unafraid.

He no longer cared why the Fates allowed her to see him. All that mattered was that she did. And she wasn't afraid of him.

Not so far anyway.

Pallidus descended. Azrael wrapped his arms tighter around Sara, knowing what lay below would not be pleasant.

Puffs of black smoke drifted past. The faint tang of sulfur tinged the air. A sharp whistle to their left, then a bright flare of light and sound.

The smoke cleared in patches, revealing the battlefield it hid. Rubble littered the streets. Bombed and blackened vehicles. Broken glass. A child's shoe.

Sara stiffened, but kept silent, pressing deeper into his embrace.

Pallidus came to rest on a patch of unbroken street, his hooves clipping against the pavement.

Sara's fingers dug into his arm. "Why are we stopping here?"

"To reap a soul." He dismounted, then offered her his hand.

She hesitated.

"Are you afraid?"

"No."

He cocked an eyebrow.

Gunfire popped in the distance. She flinched. "Yes, I'm afraid. This is a war zone. I can tell that much." A quick glance around and her gaze returned to him. Tentatively, she took his hand. "Nothing can happen to me, right?"

He nodded, absorbed in the pleasure of her willing hand in his. "I promise."

She slid to the ground beside him, staying very close.

A dark, fast-moving shadow swooped over them. She ducked, hugging tight against him. More hooves clattered on the pavement. "You said your brother was going to leave me alone."

"That isn't Kol. See?" He gestured toward the smoky gray stallion. "His horse isn't black."

She pulled back to look for herself. "Great. A new one. How many brothers do you have?"

"Only two. Chronos is a Timekeeper."

"And that means?"

"He reaps the souls of those who've reached their allotted end but have earned no special consideration or condemnation."

Ahead of them, Chronos dismounted and turned toward them. Sara sucked in a ragged breath, proof to Azrael that he wasn't the only Reaper she could see in true form. At work, Chronos most resembled the human idea of a Reaper, a skeleton cloaked in dark robes. Beneath his voluminous hood, shadows concealed all but the bottom half of a skull. Neither Azrael nor Kol were capable of assuming that form, just as Chronos couldn't assume the visceral forms unique to either of them.

Her body became one solid line pressed to his. He eased an arm around her waist, hoping to soothe her fright. She rewarded him with an almost imperceptible softening.

"Azrael." Chronos moved in their direction.

"Brother..." Azrael nodded to his brother then tipped his head at Sara, hoping to make Chronos understand the affect of his appearance.

"Ah." Flesh filled in over the bone. As he approached, he reached up and brushed his hood back, revealing his now human face.

Sara exhaled. "Your brothers are so freaking weird," she whispered.

Azrael stifled a smile. She had no idea.

Chronos stopped in front of them. He stared at Sara but spoke to Azrael. "This is the one? Interesting that you've chosen to bring her with you. Pretty, isn't she?"

"I can hear you, you know. And see you." Sara stood a little taller.

Chronos smiled and nodded to Azrael. "You're right. The Fates have it out for you."

"She saw Kol, too," Azrael added. "Saw his eyes."

Surprise registered briefly on Chronos's face. "And she didn't—"

"I stepped in before it was too late."

A pair of spiders scuttled out from the cowl of Chronos's hood to mend a frayed edge, then retreated. Sara muttered something under her breath he couldn't quite make out.

"Good that you did. I have work." Chronos pulled his hood back up, the flesh melting off his hands as he did. "Time waits for no one."

He strode off in the opposite direction of Azrael's waiting soul.

"That was completely bizarre," Sara said. "Not to mention gross and creepy."

Azrael opened his arm toward the way they need to travel. "It must be very hard to understand all of this."

Sara shook her head. "Your brother is infested with bugs. What part don't I get?"

"Those creatures are part of him."

"Great. What's your secret?" She lifted the edge of his robe. "I hate spiders, so if there's anything under there I should know about, tell me now."

Azrael bit his tongue. This was neither the time nor the place for witty repartee. "Come. A soul needs me."

* * *

The building they entered was dark enough that it took Sara's eyes a moment to adjust. Worn rugs, woven of scraps, covered the cement floor. Two wooden chairs provided the only seating. A few faded magazine pages hung pinned to the wall. Through a slim opening, the edge of thin mattress was visible, pushed up against a back wall. Was this a home, then?

Another explosion shook the walls. Bits of dust and a few chunks of debris rained down, but Sara didn't feel a thing. The fragments seemed to pass right through her.

Azrael gestured to the opening. She went ahead, watching as he came behind her. His wings folding tighter to his back as he passed through, but they still scraped the narrow passage. His eyes focused beyond her.

Covered with a tattered blanket, a young man lay on the mattress, his eyes closed, hands crossed over his body. His shirt and vest were dirty and torn, his face unshaved for days. An older man crouched on the floor beside him, rocking back and forth, praying softly in an unknown tongue.

"His father," Azrael said, gesturing toward the older man with a tip of his head. "He won't leave his son while he still lives, even though this area isn't safe and his wife and younger son wait for him in another village."

"He can't hear us or see us?" she whispered.

"No. Right now, we exist on a different plane."

She tried not to think about what that meant exactly. "Why doesn't he just carry his son out of here?"

Azrael didn't have to answer the question. The father pulled the blanket back.

A rusty stain covered the mattress beneath the younger man's torso. His clothing was torn away, revealing a dark, angry wound. The father dipped a rag in a bowl of water, rung it out and gently wiped at the injury. His son moaned.

Sara put her hand to her mouth. Liquid heat burned her eyes. "He can't move him. Would the son...pass on his own anyway?"

"Yes." Azrael's wings unfurled as much as possible in the low-ceilinged room. "But it is better that I take the son now, sparing him further pain and setting the father free to reunite with his remaining family."

He looked at her, holding her gaze with his dark one. "You understand this? What I do?"

She nodded. She understood perfectly. He was truly the Angel of Death. The Reaper of Mercy. And knowing who he was only made her like him that much more. A man who put the needs of others first. Who cared about people's pain and suffering.

So his brothers were scary and creepy. Manda's younger brother worked as a female impersonator and she didn't have a problem with it. Sara could learn to deal.

The father finished tending his son and recovered him, returning to his prayerful rocking. In the distance, gunfire echoed like corn popping.

Azrael stepped away from her and stood beside the father. He reached down and took the son's hand, pulling a wavering, transparent likeness of the son to his feet.

The likeness stared at Azrael, then at his father. He mumbled something, nodded to Azrael, and then drifted into nothing.

The father's head came up. The rocking stopped. He laid a hand on his son's shoulder. "Emir?" He shook his son gently. "Emir?" His voice was louder this time.

He laid his head to his son's chest and went very still. After a few moments, he closed his eyes and began to weep.

Azrael turned, blocking her sight with his wings. "Our time here is up."

Sara rose up on her tiptoes, trying to see the father. "Will he be okay? Will he get out of here safely?"

"I don't know. I can't see the future, only what I'm given." He lifted his hand toward the doorway. "We must go."

Pallidus was right where they'd left him. This time, Azrael helped Sara up first, then settled in behind her. She wanted to say something to him, to tell him that even though everything he'd shown her had been horrific, she understood that he wasn't responsible for the people's deaths. She saw clearly what his role was and how good he was. How kind.

But as they ascended, she just couldn't find the words. None of the sentences forming in her head seemed to fully capture what she felt, or what she wanted to tell him about everything she'd seen. And the way she understood who he was and what he did.

Maybe he knew. Maybe words weren't necessary.

She leaned back a little, just enough to feel the hard wall of muscle behind her. Ray always told her she was a lousy communicator. That he never understood what she was thinking.

Clouds spread out like a field of snow beneath them. No way of telling how quickly this experience would end.

"Azrael?"

"Yes?" His voice sounded from near her ear, as though his head was dipped to be closer to her. One simple word and she nearly shivered with the delicious things it did to her. He spoke it so it meant a million more things. Like he was offering himself to her.

She dismissed the heady fantasy that a being like this could want her. He could have any woman. Probably did. Still, she wouldn't give up this opportunity since she'd had so few recently.

"Thank you...for taking me with you. It wasn't easy to see a lot of what you showed me, but I understand now. About you. And what you do." There was so much more, but she couldn't bring herself to say how wonderful it would be to see him again without sounding like some foolish, lovesick teenager and she really didn't want to look foolish in front of him.

He was silent for longer than she'd expected. Crap. Had she said something to offend him?

"I'm glad," he said, instantly relieving her. "I apologize if my brothers frightened you."

She laughed softly. "You can't choose your family."

"Sometimes you can."

Tipping her head, she glanced up. He was looking straight ahead, his eyes unreadable. "What does that mean?"

"Nothing." He shook his head. "We're almost back."

The clouds rose up around them, obscuring her view. When they cleared, Pallidus stood in the hospital hallway where they'd started out.

Azrael slid down and held out his hands to help her. She reached for him, settling her hands on his solid shoulders, his hands grasping her waist. Bittersweet warmth filled her in that moment knowing they'd already begun to say goodbye.

The time they'd just spent together had been interesting a way she could never explain to any of her friends. More than that, the sense of calm she felt being with him...no man had ever made her feel that way.

No man.

Her hands slipped from his shoulders and down his arms as her feet touched linoleum. How amazing those eyes were...obsidian and silver and magic. His hands stayed at her waist, which was fine with her. Death was much warmer than she'd have guessed.

"I guess this is goodbye then." She bent her head to stare at his chest and the weave of his robe.

His grip loosened. "Only if...yes, I guess it is." His hands fell away.

She looked up as her hands went to her sides. "I won't see you anymore?"

Lines bracketed his mouth. "I don't know how long your ability to see me will be allowed."

"Allowed? Who's allowing me to see you now?" She propped her fists on her hips.

"The Fates." He rolled his eyes heavenward, shaking his head in obvious disgust.

"You mean like the Greek mythology Fates?"

"Something like that, yes." He sighed.

"Are you telling me they're real, too?"

He nodded. "Unfortunately."

She raised her brows. "Not your favorite people, I take it?"

"Let's just say we don't always see eye to eye."

Sara tipped her head back. "We don't either." That got her a smile. A bright, knee-melting smile.

"And yet you might be my most favorite person of all."

Now would be a good time for him to kiss her. Especially since she might never ever see him again. "What if I don't agree with the Fates either?"

His forehead wrinkled. "What do you mean?"

"What if they don't want me to see you again, but I do?"

New light sparkled in his eyes. "You want to see me?"

"It's...kind of neat to be able to see you." That was lame, but telling him she thought he was hot was out of the question. Better stick to the sheer novelty of being friends with the Angel of Death, for now. She shrugged as nonchalantly as she could manage. "You could stop by when you're not, you know, reaping souls. Say hi, that kind of thing."

He sighed. Seeming to deflate a bit. "Oh. Sure."

Ray was right. She was a horrible communicator. She laid her hand on Azrael's arm. "What I mean to say is that I...like you. And I'd like to see you again." She paused. "I want to see you again. If that's okay with you."

A smile curved his full mouth. "You're asking me on a date."

"No!" She slapped her hands over her face. "Yes." She peeked from between her fingers. "Is that even possible? You and me dating, I mean?"

"I don't see why not."

"What about you being invisible to everyone else? You don't think that might be an issue?" She could see it now. Having imaginary friends as a child was one thing, but imaginary dates? Not a good idea. Manda would have her signed into the psych ward in a hot minute.

He leaned forward, eyes twinkling with something new. "I have a human form. No one will know who I really am except for you."

"Really?" Hope sprung eternal.

"Yes, really."

"So I guess we could go out then. At least once. I mean, we could try it." Her hands started trembling. She took a deep breath and tried not to think too much about what had just happened. But then, her first date in seven months was a night out with the Angel of Death. A little trepidation was to be expected.

She twisted her hands, bit at the inside of her cheek. "How do we do this? I'm guessing you don't have a phone or email."

He gave her a little half-smile. "Freeman Square, the general's statue, seven o'clock. I'll take care of the rest."

"You know Freeman Square?"

"I know a lot of places."

She bet he did. "Seven o'clock tomorrow?"

"Is that all right?"

"Yes." She'd find a way to be there. Maybe switch shifts with another secretary. "I'll be there." She was going on a date. With Death. Even her skin felt twitchy now.

He laid a hand on Pallidus' shoulder. "I'm looking forward to it."

"Me too." And she meant it, despite the new nerves.

Mounting in a smooth, easy motion, he nodded to her as the fog lifted, obscuring him. A few seconds later, the mist cleared and he was gone.

Feeling a bit fuzzy-headed, she blinked a few times before realizing she was technically still at work. She wandered down the hall, back to the nurse's station.

Manda's head popped up. "Done practicing your Tai Bo?"

She narrowed her eyes as if looking serious might add some veracity to her statement. "I was getting water."

Manda looked at Sara's hands. "So where is it?"

"I didn't have any singles."

"You want to borrow a dollar?" Manda's cheeks bunched in a poorly contained smile.

Smarty pants. "No, I'm good." Water was the last thing on her mind.

"You want to go over those schedules now?"

"Sure," Sara answered. Manda acted like nothing unusual had happened. Sara glanced at the clock.

She'd only been gone three minutes.

Chapter Six

"Kol!"

Azrael bellowed his brother's name into the cold wind that perpetually scrubbed Kol's bleak domain, trying to be heard above the reverberating thump of the mortal music Kol constantly played. Shades drifted past, plucking at him, searching for remnants of souls to make their own.

Kol's front door stayed closed, but the music's pounding increased. Calling it music was being kind. Mortals named it heavy metal. Azrael knew his brother played it to drown out the cries of the reaped souls he heard day in and day out. So be it. Azrael had no room in his heart for sympathy today.

"Kol! I know you're in there." The Reapers could sense each other. "Let me in or I'll break the door down."

The door didn't move. With no servants to open it, Kol would have to do it himself. Azrael growled low in his throat as he stomped up the stairs and onto Kol's porch. His brother's lack of hospitality was completely understandable, but did nothing to temper Azrael's anger over his recent behavior.

"This is your last chance." He pounded his fist on the door. "Let me in."

Azrael knew how his brothers saw him. Because he was the Reaper of Mercy, they imagined him the weakest of the three. Slow to anger, quick to forgive, always there when they needed him. Certainly no one they should worry about. Time for them to think differently.

Time for them to understand *that* Azrael was gone.

He leaned back, lifted his foot and kicked the door open, splintering the casing and yanking the hinges loose with a metallic screech audible above the sound of mortal rock and roll.

"Kol!"

The music died away. A pale shadow emerged at the top of the sweeping stairway. "That was unnecessary."

Shirtless in black leather pants, Kol had obviously just rolled out of his bed, no doubt recovering from some debauchery. His dark glasses were missing as well. He shoved a hand through his long black hair and stared hard at Azrael, although his fatal gaze only worked on mortals.

Azrael stared back. "Your actions toward my female companion were unacceptable."

"Female companion." Kol laughed derisively and shook his head. "You're such a snob, Az. Maybe getting some will lighten you up, but I doubt it."

Heat gnawed at Azrael's belly. "And being like you would be better? Perhaps you're right, but nights of indiscriminate sex with mortal women too drunk to understand who I am just isn't my style."

Kol's eyes flashed. "I don't have a choice."

"You could choose not to."

"Get out of my house." Kol headed toward his bedroom.

"Not until you swear to leave Sara alone."

Kol turned, eyes narrowing. "Or what? You'll huff and you'll puff and blow my house down? Go home, Az. You don't scare me."

The Darkness rose within him, a razor-clawed dragon awakening hungry after eons of sleep. He gave it sway, let it fill him.

"Don't I?" The words left him in a guttural snarl.

Kol stepped back, jutted his chin out. "Our visceral forms take ages to master. You can't threaten me with something you have no control over."

Taking advantage of Kol's large entryway, Azrael unfurled his wings to their full span. Neither Chronos nor Kol had ever seen his full visceral form, but Kol's words pushed him to reveal more.

Talons sprouted from the joints of his gray-feathered wings. The Darkness surged along his veins, twisted over his bones like a poison vine. It craved full release. Azrael held it in check. This was not the time.

"Your assumptions will be your ruin, brother." The Darkness turned his voice to gravel. Giving it full reign would erase his voice altogether. "Leave Sara alone or I will prove how wrong you are."

Kol nodded, his unshaded eyes large. His lips parted, but no sound came out.

The look on Kol's face was answer enough. Azrael swept through Kol's ruined door. An uncommon happiness filled him. He smiled as The Darkness retreated.

His date with Sara couldn't come soon enough.

* * *

Sara threw the third outfit of the afternoon onto the bed. As if getting out of work early wasn't hard enough, now she had to figure out what to wear. How was she supposed to do that when she didn't know what they'd be doing or where they'd be going on their date?

A smile played on her lips. They were going on a date. If she'd had the time, she would have gone shopping for something new. Her cable bill could wait another week.

She grabbed her favorite little black dress. The three-quarter length sleeves and wrap styling made it a classic, but she'd hesitated to try it, wondering if it was too dressy. One twirl in the mirror and she couldn't think of a better outfit.

Silver filigree hoops and black peep-toe heels completed the look. *Please don't let him show up in jeans and a t-shirt when I look like this.* Maybe he'd wear khaki's and a nice shirt. Or better yet...a suit. A man in a suit made her knees weak. The thought of Azrael in one made her nearly faint and more than a little hot.

She fanned herself. Time enough for fantasies later. The real thing was waiting for her.

She grabbed one of her favorite vintage finds, an ivory cardigan with jet beading. The nights were getting cooler and they might go for a walk. She liked the idea of that, especially if it were hand-in-hand.

Her small silver mesh handbag only held a few essentials but when it came to dating the Angel of Death, choosing lipstick over pepper spray seemed like a no-brainer. Besides, if he were going to try something, wouldn't he have done it already?

Another smile curved her mouth as she slicked on raspberry gloss. He *would* try something, wouldn't he? Like at least a kiss?

Half an hour later, she'd finally found parking within two blocks of Freeman Square. She popped a breath mint before she got out, then locked her little red compact. The car might not be sexy, but it was reliable and good on gas. And the only thing she'd been able to afford after the divorce.

She checked her reflection in the car window, smoothing her hair and wishing for something more exciting than straight and mouse-brown. Nothing to be done about it now.

A few couples strolled through Freeman Square as dusk settled. A young man in a knit cap and goatee played guitar on the steps of the bandstand.

She'd come here with Ray once, early on in their relationship. It was one of the few happy memories she had of their time together. Before she'd realized how controlling he could be.

The melody of running water told her she was almost at her destination. The general's statue was the centerpiece of the park's fountain.

Fresh nerves tingled over her skin. She checked her watch. Early by ten minutes. Would he be there yet? What did his human form look like? What had he planned? Would he think she looked nice?

Deep breath. Dating was dating, no matter how much time passed between actual occurrences. Of course, she'd never dated a supernatural being before. She smiled. Maybe he was nervous too.

Somehow, she doubted it.

* * *

Azrael materialized in the midst of some trees where he couldn't be seen. With only a second's concentration, he changed into his human form. It had been a while since he'd taken it on. He hadn't had the desire.

Still, the human male was an enjoyable form to assume. He stretched, feeling the way his muscles moved. Being human was a pleasure he'd denied himself, thinking it would drive him to the same kind of pursuits his brothers enjoyed. At least tonight, he would not have to worry about that. Sara wanted his company. If things went well tonight, she would continue to feel that way.

He straightened his jacket, wondering what she'd think of him. His human appearance differed a bit from the way he looked as a Reaper. What if she didn't like it? Or didn't recognize him?

He groaned softly. Maybe this was a bad idea. How did Chronos and Kol do it? But he knew how. Knew enough anyway, to know he was nothing like them. The women they mixed with meant nothing to them, where as he, in a small way, already cared for Sara.

She made him feel alive. No one had ever done that.

He stepped out onto the path. Ahead of him strolled another man who appeared to be about the age of Azrael's human form. He carried a large bouquet of pink roses. Azrael looked at his own pitifully empty hands.

He'd brought her nothing.

Cursing himself for the oversight, he wondered what gift might be suitable. Flowers wouldn't do this time. Carrying them around all night could become a chore for her, and by the end of the evening, they'd be wilted. Something smaller, more meaningful.

He glanced around, but the people who were out paid him no attention. He ducked back into the bushes, took Reaper form, plucked a feather from each of his wings, then changed back to mortal form. Closing his hands palms together over the feathers, he pictured the perfect gift. He glanced around. No one seemed to notice the quick flash of light. Opening his hands, he nodded and smiled.

Now, if only she liked it. He tucked the surprise into his pocket and headed for the statue.

* * *

Sara sat on the thick marble edge circling the fountain's pool. A single star twinkled in the faded purple sky. She gazed up at the night, her nerves ebbing away with the peacefulness of it all.

Tonight, she'd live in the moment. Tomorrow could worry about itself. She deserved an evening of fun.

"Sara?"

Reverie broken, she turned and looked into the face of the most gorgeous man she'd ever seen. Azrael. She knew him instantly, even though his hair was now jet-black, his eyes no longer sparkled chrome. Everything about him was sharper and more beautiful. As if a layer of dust had been wiped from his image.

"Azrael," she whispered his name, suddenly unsure of herself. Maybe he went by another name in this form. She took in his black suit, the crisp white shirt open at the neck. It might be illegal for a man to look that good.

He smiled and extended his hand to help her up. She didn't trust her legs to support her with him looking like this, but took his hand anyway.

She rose and he pulled her close. "You look beautiful, my Sara."

Flutters of excitement and his achingly male scent stirred her blood. "Thanks. So do you. Look handsome, I mean." She laughed softly, letting a few of her nerves escape.

"I'm nervous," she confessed. Why not be honest? After what he'd shared with her, there seemed no reason not to be.

Concern shadowed his eyes. "Why? Did you think I wouldn't show?"

"No...no, I knew you'd be here." She had to look away for a moment, catch her breath. She wasn't used to so much male attention focused solely on her. Inhaling, she started over. "I haven't been on a date in a long time."

His smile sparked a calming heat in her belly. He leaned in to whisper in her ear. "I haven't been on a date ever."

She pulled back to look him in the eyes. "Ever? As in never ever?"

He dipped his head. Was that embarrassment on his face? "No."

"Wow." How could that be? She was the first woman he'd ever been out with. Was she the first woman he'd asked, or the first woman he'd said yes to? Either way, it was pretty cool to be Death's first date. "Well, I have to admit that makes me feel a little better." She grinned. "Actually, it makes me feel pretty special."

"You are special." He slipped his hand into his jacket pocket. "I brought you something."

"You did? I didn't bring you anything."

His brow crinkled. "Is it customary for the woman to bring her date a gift?"

"Not really, I guess, but presents should be reciprocated."

He shook his head. "There is no need. All I want is time with you." He held his hand up, dangling something sparkly in the evening light.

She got a better look and sucked in a breath. To say this was completely unexpected would be an understatement.

"I hope you like it. I wanted to give you something to remind you of me."

"I'm not about to forget you, trust me." She lifted the necklace against her palm. A delicate pair of wings glittered at the end of a fine spun silver chain. They arched together in an abstract heart shape, the lines of every feather perfect. She almost expected the pendant to be soft to the touch. "It's beautiful. Incredible."

A smile broke across his face. "You like it?"

"I love it. I want to wear it right now." She turned her back to him and lifted her hair, looking over her shoulder. "Will you help me?"

He placed the necklace around her throat, his fingers brushing the back of her neck as he secured the clasp. Goosebumps raced down her arms with the pleasure of the brief touch.

"There."

She turned back to face him, positioning the wings so they hung at the hollow of her throat. "How does it look?"

His eyes never left hers. "Beautiful."

She understood he wasn't talking about the necklace. She smiled and heat washed over her skin. "Thank you." An entirely inadequate response. She'd rather kiss him, but making the first move might freak him out. She didn't want his first date to be his last. Not with her anyway. If he never dated another woman, that was fine with her.

He cleared his throat and smoothed a crease she couldn't see in the lapel of his jacket. "I know that dating protocol requires certain...actions...be reserved for the end of the evening, but I don't feel like waiting."

"What?" She studied the breadth of his hands while trying to figure out what he was talking about. What would those hands feel like on her—

"Sara."

She looked up. "Yes?"

"I'm trying to say..." His voice dropped an octave. "I want to kiss you. Now."

The breath left her body and her stomach dropped to the bottom of her feet. She froze to the spot, her tongue useless.

Yes. Yes. Yes!

Nod. She could nod.

So she did.

Chapter Seven

"Does that mean you give me permission?" Hope lit his delicious face. If he got any better looking, she'd faint dead away.

"Uh-huh," she squeaked out.

"Good," he breathed. "Because I didn't plan on asking twice."

One step forward and his hands threaded through her hair, spreading warmth to parts south. He tilted her face to meet his. Their bodies met in a hot, seamless press. She couldn't breathe and didn't care. Nothing mattered but the here and now. His hands, his body, his mouth.

Her fingers splayed against his chest. Hot. Hard. Hers.

He kissed her with a fierceness that melted any remaining thought. His hunger brought her to life. Made her want.

Made her need.

She slid her arms beneath his jacket, wrapping them around his steely torso. Desire washed through her, leaving her breathless and open. Nothing compared to this man, this kiss. Not any joy she'd ever known.

And in that moment, she knew she would do anything to make this last.

One hand stayed cradling her head, the other drifted to the small of her back and pressed her closer. His fingers kneaded her skin. Sparks skittered along her spine, igniting white-hot pinpoints of sensation all over her body. Another minute of this and she would combust.

All control disappeared. She dug her fingers into his sides, urging, pleading...she wanted more. Whatever he had to give, she wanted. Her tongue found his, flicking across his teeth.

With a moan low in his throat, he broke the kiss. His chest rose and fell with the effort to breathe. His eyes glinted raw yearning and something darker, something animal.

"Sara..." His lips stayed parted as he drank in air.

She couldn't focus on anything but his mouth. The fullness of his bottom lip. She wanted to sink her teeth into it.

She blinked, exhaled, tried to remind herself they were in the middle of Freeman Square. "That was..."

Another exhale. She couldn't find the right word. What had he done to her?

A new thought struck her. If this was his first date... "That wasn't your first kiss, was it?"

He licked his lips. "Yes. Was it that obvious?"

"I think I'm in trouble." Seriously. His first kiss? It had nearly made her lose her mind. "It wasn't obvious at all."

"It was all right then?"

"It was more than all right. It was the best kiss I've ever had."

He smiled, shifting from one foot to the other. "Mine too." He laughed. "That was not a smart thing to say, but it's true."

She laughed along with him. The feeling was just coming back to her extremities. She glanced around, surprised they hadn't drawn a crowd of gawkers. "I feel a little dumb right now myself."

He slipped his hand into hers. The warmth helped her reconnect to reality. They had a whole night ahead of them.

"Are you hungry?" he asked.

"Yes." For him. "What did you have in mind?"

He dropped her hand and offered the crook of his arm. She laced her arm through his, snuggling next to him.

"You'll see," he said with a wink, leading her toward the town center.

They strolled in companionable silence until he brought them to a stop in front of Pétrus, a fashionable French restaurant with a reputation for romance. More proposals happened at Pétrus than any other restaurant in town. She ought to know. Ray had proposed here.

Azrael reached for the door, smiling and obviously pleased with his choice. His smile faded when he looked at her.

"What's wrong?"

"Nothing." She faked a smile in return.

"You're lying." His jaw tightened and he let the door swing shut. "Please tell me what's bothering you, Sara."

She shrugged. "I don't want to ruin your evening."

Gently, he rested his hands on her shoulders. "This is our evening. If you don't like this restaurant, we can go somewhere else."

She was being silly, but she couldn't help herself. She didn't want to make any memories with Azrael in a place that was part of her old life. "Are you sure?"

"Positive." His jaw relaxed. "Is the food no good here?"

Laughing, she shook her head. "It's very good...I just have memories here...with someone else..."

"Oh." He turned away but not before she saw the stricken look on his face.

"Wait." She grabbed his forearm.

He stopped, stared at the sidewalk.

"Let me explain."

"No need. I understand." Hard lines creased his forehead.

"I don't think you do—"

His gaze burned into her. "Why did you kiss me if you're involved with someone else?"

That got them a few turned heads and a raised eyebrow from the passersby.

She lowered her voice and stepped closer. "I'm not involved with anyone else." She sighed. "My ex-husband proposed to me here. I just didn't want to be with you in a place that had bad memories for me. It was silly, I know. We can eat here, really. I'll be fine."

He lifted her hands to his mouth and pressed a kiss to them. "My apologies for assuming otherwise. I am the fool. Forgive me?"

"Of course," she said. "Wait, no."

His eyes widened. "No?"

"Not unless you kiss me again." The words were barely audible but she got them out. She wanted another kiss and she didn't care who saw it.

His mouth found hers before another thought entered her head. This time, he kissed her more deliberately, slower, as though he mapped every nuance of her mouth, trying to sear it into his mind.

She moaned softly. His tongue swept hers. The taste of him swirled through her, a sweet, heady smoke.

A wolf whistle separated them in laughter.

"Now am I forgiven?" His eyes sparkled like he hoped she said no again.

"For now." She grinned and drew her finger down his chest. Forget dinner, she wanted dessert.

"I am willing to try again."

"Duly noted and much appreciated." Heaven help her, but she could get used to this.

She moved toward the restaurant's door. Azrael could provide her with new memories.

He tugged her back to his side. "I know a better place."

"Are you sure? It's okay, really."

"You deserve better than okay. Come." He tipped his head, drawing her down the street.

"Where are we going?"

"Somewhere else."

She laughed. "I figured that."

He ushered her onto a side street, then into an alley. He whistled low and long. Pallidus walked toward them from a drift of fog.

"I'm guessing wherever we're going, it's not local."

Azrael scrubbed Pallidus' neck. "No, it's not, but it will be worth the trip."

"I'm not really dressed for horseback."

"I'll hold you in my lap."

Who could say no to that? "Okay."

A curl of mist wound up from his feet, covering him as it rose. When it cleared, he was the winged Reaper she'd first met once again. "I can't travel in my human form. I'll change back when we arrive."

"Good. I like you in a suit."

He mounted Pallidus, then reached for her. He set her in his lap, her legs across his, her bottom firmly planted between his thighs.

She couldn't resist brushing her fingers through his hair before clasping her hands around his neck. The move made her flush. "Soft," she murmured.

He bent to kiss her again, and when she opened her eyes clouds surrounded them.

"Where are we going?" Not that she cared. Anywhere with him would be fine with her.

"You'll see soon enough." He tightened his arm around her waist. A myriad of emotions showed in his mesmerizing gaze.

"What's on your mind?" she asked. She wanted to know this man, wanted to understand him.

A slight smile appeared and disappeared. "I don't know where to start."

"At the beginning?"

He smiled again, shook his head. "It's not that easy."

She shrugged and moved her hands around his waist so she could lean against his chest. "You'll find a place to start when you're ready."

"I like you, Sara Donovan."

A pleased smile teased her lips up. She closed her eyes and turned her face into the crook of his neck, brushing her lips across his warm skin.

"I like you, too, Azrael...whatever your last name is."

"Grim," he answered. "Azrael Grim."

"Appropriate," she whispered against his skin. He shivered and her pleasure at his response filled her with a sense of empowerment never felt before.

Azrael might be the Angel of Death, but he'd made her fall in love with life all over again.

* * *

"We're almost there," Azrael whispered to the lovely creature curled on his lap. He'd already had Pallidus

94

circle the city twice to keep her snuggled against him a little longer. He craved her warmth and perfume like they were drugs.

She stretched, arching against him. He kissed her temple.

Something terrible and wonderful had happened between them already this night. The thought of being without her made him ache and the evening had just begun.

She filled the long empty parts of him. Made his heart beat with purpose. Gave his breath reason. He wanted her, not just in the way a man wanted a woman, but in the way of a being who'd never before understood the possibilities of a future no longer alone.

Companion.

The word kept repeating in his brain. Was such a thing even possible? He couldn't think about the chance it wasn't.

"Wherever we are, it looks beautiful." She leaned forward, watching the cloud cover fray beneath them. "So many lights...it looks like a fairy land."

Pallidus went lower still. She clapped a hand over her mouth, then pointed. "Is that...it is! The Eiffel Tower!" She turned to him, eyes filled with amazement. "We're in Paris?"

"Since Pétrus was out, I thought we'd go right to the source." Pleasing her could easily become his life's work, so long as she always looked at him that way.

She shook her head. "I can't believe it. I've never been out of the state." Her fingers pressed to her mouth, she kept her gaze on the rising city.

"So beautiful," she whispered again. Her hand crept down to find his. She wove their finger together, squeezing tight. "I don't know what to say." She looked over her shoulder, eyes bright with unshed tears. "Thank you."

Pallidus set down in a vacant back street and they dismounted. Another curl of fog and Azrael retook his human form.

"Shall we?" He offered her his arm and together they wandered the streets of Paris until Sara's growling stomach stopped them at a small café.

They ate at a sidewalk table, sitting side by side, laughing, talking and drinking wine. Sara's fascination with the Parisians walking by kept him smiling. Seeing things through her eyes made him realize how good life was.

"Look at her." She tapped his arm. "Her dog's collar matches her purse. They certainly have a sense of style, don't they?"

He nodded, but truthfully, he had a hard time seeing anyone but her. She was incredible. A bright shining star to his perpetual twilight. He kissed her fingers, knowing it would make her smile.

"You're a very sweet man." She dipped her head. A curtain of chestnut silk swung around her shoulders, hiding her hazel eyes. If he painted, she would be the only subject he ever needed.

"You're a very beautiful woman."

She blushed, shaking her head. "You're just flattering me. I'm okay, but not beautiful."

"No. Flattery implies falsehoods and I would never lie to you." He caught her gaze and held it, trying to make her see the truth in his eyes. "You *are* beautiful, Sara."

All traces of happiness left her face. "It's nice that you think that, but I don't feel that way." She twisted her fingers out of his grasp and wrapped her arms around her body. "I've been in this skin for thirty-two years. I know I'm not beautiful."

He moved closer and cradled her face in his hands. "But you are. And anyone who's made you think otherwise is a fool." He brushed his mouth across hers. "I would be happy to help you forget them."

She laughed lightly and covered his hands with hers. "They've already begun to fade." She kissed him back, her berry-flavored tongue teasing his. She sighed, a wonderful sound of soul-deep pleasure.

"Maybe we should think about getting back." Otherwise, he was going to take her to the nearest hotel and spend the rest of the night giving her reasons to make that sound again. That was as long as he could keep the Darkness under control. She called to that part of him with an almost undeniable fierceness.

"Already?" She looked at her watch. "I guess you're right. The Eiffel Tower's probably been closed for hours."

"We saw it on our way here."

"I know, but I'd love to stand up there and look out over the city. Seems like a very romantic thing to do." She shrugged. "Shame to come all this way and not, you know?"

"I agree." He stood and extended his hand. "Let's go. I think it's open into the evening hours."

She took his hand and stood, then looked at the remains of their meal. "Don't we need to pay for this?"

He dug in his pocket and pulled out a stack of bills.

"Wow, that's a lot of money. But it's all American—" she fell silent as the dollars changed to euros in his hand. "How did you do that?"

He smiled and tossed enough to cover the bill on the table. "I have many talents."

And when the right opportunity presented itself, he was going to show her.

Repeatedly.

Chapter Eight

"I knew the view from here would be amazing. Look at this place...it's like a fairy tale." Sara leaned back against Azrael. His arms wrapped her tight, filling her with the sensation that the sea of twinkling lights below them was somehow a manifestation of her happiness.

Standing on the top observation deck of the Eiffel Tour was something she'd never thought she'd get to do. The fact that it had been closed for half an hour made no difference to Azrael. In his Reaper form, he'd simply held her close and moments later, here they stood.

He was amazing in every aspect. The way he treated her, the way he looked at her. Told her she was beautiful. She could get used to this man. Who was she kidding? She was already falling for him.

And he was fluent in French. She had a feeling he could speak any language necessary, but he oozed sexy when he spoke French.

"Say something in French again," she whispered, half-embarrassed to ask.

"What would you like me to say?"

"I don't care if you read the phone book, I just like the way it sounds."

He laughed softly and drew her closer. He was silent for a moment before he spoke.

"*Comment t'exprimer tout ce que je ressens? Ton image hante mes nuits. Je suis affamé pour vous.*"

"Mmmm. That sounds nice. What does it mean?"

"You didn't say I had to translate."

"C'mon, I want to know."

"It means...the night is beautiful and so are you."

"I thought the word for beautiful was belle?" She tipped her head to look at him. "Didn't you tell me at dinner that you'd never lie to me?"

"I wasn't lying. It was more like keeping a secret."

She twisted in his arms so she could see him face to face. "What did you say?"

"Some things I probably shouldn't have."

"Now I really want to know." She waggled her brows. "Were you talking dirty to me?"

"Would that work?"

Grinning, she cuffed his shoulder. "You're wicked."

"It's good that you've figured that out."

"It is? Why?"

His hands slipped from her waist to grasp her hips in a move that was pure animal possession. "Because I'm full of wicked thoughts. About you."

A shiver rolled down her spine. "You are?"

"Yes." His eyes gleamed bright, predatory. Wanton.

Her pulse sped up. "I think you're the man my mother warned me about."

"Really. Did she tell you I might do this?" His hands went lower. He cupped her buttocks, crushing her against him. "Or this?" His teeth nipped her neck, followed by his tongue. He nibbled a path to her ear, hot breath tormenting her, making her writhe.

"Never mentioned it..." she murmured.

"You've lit a fire in me, Sara. I need you. I can't imagine being without you, even after knowing you for so short a time." He breathed deeply. "I want you in my life, but I also know it isn't fair for you."

He released her. Cool air rushed in between them.

"What isn't fair?" She wanted him. Regardless.

"I'm not a normal man, Sara. I don't live in your world. I can't be a part of your life like an ordinary mortal. This..." He gestured to himself. "This isn't who I am. And if I don't take this form, no one else can see me. It's no way for you to live."

"So you take your human form more often."

Turning half away, he dragged his hand through his hair, tousling the black waves. "You deserve more. Someone who can be there for you all the time."

"I'd be happy with whatever time you could give me." After the passion he'd just shown her, was he trying to say this was goodbye? She clutched the pendant he'd given her. "I don't want to stop seeing you."

He stared out into the Parisian night as if looking for answers.

"Azrael."

He closed his eyes, letting his chin drop to his chest. "It's better we part now, before this becomes something we both regret."

The Angel of Death had apparently lost his mind. She decided to give him a piece of hers. She stepped forward and grabbed his arm. "No."

He slanted his eyes at her. The edge of chrome was there for a second, then gone. "No?"

She held onto him more tightly. "I refuse."

He blinked and lifted his head. "You refuse." His jaw shifted to one side, his expression pensive. "I'm a Reaper. No one talks to me like that."

She let go of him and lifted her chin. "Well, maybe it's about time."

Straightening to his full height, he faced her, a new gleam in his eyes. "I don't think you should have said that."

She stepped back. "W-why?"

"Because." He advanced so quickly she didn't see him move. "Now I want you more than ever."

He reached for her, then dropped his hands, fisting them at his sides. His face contorted...with pain, anger, lust...she couldn't tell. A low growl emanated from him. He fought something, that much she understood.

"This can't be, Sara. No matter how brave you think you are...you have no idea what I truly am."

She held her ground. "Yes, I do. You collect men's souls. I've seen it. Been with you while you did it. I'm not afraid."

A humorless laugh echoed off the steel platform. "You wouldn't say that if you saw what hides in me."

Swallowing down her fear, she stood tall. She'd called his bluff once. She could do it again. "Then show me."

He shook his head, hands still fisted, eyes heavy-lidded. His mouth twisted. "You don't know what you ask."

"Show me and let me decide for myself."

Again, he shook his head. "No. It's just one more reason we shouldn't see each other anymore. You bring out the Darkness in me." He retreated, knowing she wouldn't understand, needing to protect her. "The more I'm with you, the more I want you." Another step back. "The more afraid I am I won't be able to contain it."

"I want you, too, Azrael." Bold words, but she meant them.

He raised his hand as if he could block her words. "Don't say that. I need to regain control. Already I feel it rise within—"

"Kiss me, Azrael." She walked toward him.

"Stop," he nearly begged. He backed into a stanchion and wheeled around like someone had touched him. When he faced her again, his irises were almost completely engulfed in blue flame.

A calmness she'd never felt before washed through her, erasing her fear. He wouldn't hurt her. She believed that. More than anything, she wanted to comfort him, to show him he was worth caring about, no matter how awful he thought he was.

In the twinkling darkness, she came to him and took his face in her hands. His skin burned.

"Don't fear this," she whispered, leaning toward him.

She held nothing back, pouring every desire she'd had for him into the crush of her mouth. With her lips on his, she played out the images in her head. Their bodies entwined, slick with sweat. His possession of her. Her willful submission. With her tongue, she revealed her desire. Her want. Her need.

He kissed her back, his moans growing louder, deeper. His hands clutched at her until he drew her against him so tightly her head spun.

Fabric tore.

His skin cooled.

He shoved her away, covering his face with his arm as he retreated further beneath the structure. "Don't come any closer. I can't...stop it..."

She didn't know which he was now, human or Reaper. Then it became clearer.

Wings sprouted from his back, but they weren't the wings she'd seen before. Spines tipped the joints and drapes of shadow replaced the feathers.

More tearing. Mist expanded around him, blurring her vision. Then it split down the middle, spiraling away in thick whorls.

He stepped through, shedding his human form like a discarded chrysalis. Her calm leaked away.

Gone was the man she knew. In his place stood a wraith of shadows and fog. His robe lost shape past the shoulders, dissolving into shards of mist and twilight. Beneath the hood two fiery blue eyes bored into her from a fathomless blackness.

"Azrael?" In this state, did he still know who she was? She felt behind her for the railing, moving back a step.

He glided toward her, one tendril of mist lifting, reaching...

She exhaled a shuddering breath, racking her brain for something to say or do. He came closer. Another tendril drifted in her direction.

With nothing to lose, she let go of the railing and stepped toward him.

His forward movement slowed.

"I'm not afraid you," she lied, searching for bravado she wasn't sure she had.

"So what if you have this other side." She shrugged to keep from shivering. "You should see me first thing in the morning. It's not pretty, believe me."

The reaching strands of fog dissolved.

New resolve empowered her. "It doesn't change the way I feel about Azrael the man and Azrael the Reaper, either. I like those aspects of you very much."

Misty threads twisted together. A faint outline of his robe emerged from the shadows.

She edged closer. "If this is your attempt to scare me away because you think I should be with a mortal man, it's not going to work." She rolled her eyes. "Been there, done that, have the divorce papers to prove it."

Translucent feathers covered his wings, solidifying as they spread.

She crossed her arms and tilted her head trying to look nonchalant, even though her heart's thumping filled her ears. "And as far as I'm concerned, you'd better snap out of it because you still owe me dessert."

The cobalt glow in his eyes dimmed and the remaining mist disappeared like a vacuum had sucked it up. Azrael, in Reaper form, stood before her.

He pushed the hood of his robe back. The only blue in his eyes was the familiar edge around his irises. He stayed silent, his gaze fixed on the ground, the muscles in his jaw flexing.

At last, he lifted his head and looked at her.

"You amaze me, Sara Donovan. How is it that you are braver than my brothers who back down at only a hint of what you saw?" He shook his head.

"I get like that when I haven't had chocolate."

A welcome smile shattered his solemn expression. "You can have all the chocolate you want." He laughed softly. "You can have anything it is in my power to give you."

She smiled back. "Are you going to provide me with a list, or should I just start guessing?"

He spanned the space between them in one step, sending a rush of heat through her. "It would take ages to tell you everything."

"Then there better be a second date," she whispered as his arms went around her.

He lifted her hand to his mouth and feathered tiny kisses over the sensitive skin on the inside of her wrist. "That's definitely within my power."

She leaned against him, relieved to have him back. "I'm not letting you off the hook about the chocolate, you know."

Nibbling his way toward the crook of her elbow, he paused to answer. "I didn't expect you would."

A breathless sigh escaped her lips as his kisses moved to just below her ear. "That's kind of...my...*oh*...weak spot."

"Then I shouldn't stop." He put an inch of space between them. "But I have to tell you how much your willingness to sacrifice yourself means to me."

"My willingness to what?" The fog of pleasure lifted.

"Your willingness to sacrifice your life. When you stood up to me in my visceral form."

"Sacrifice my life?" She swallowed.

He looked at her with sudden understanding. "You didn't know, did you?"

She shifted out of his arms a little. "What are you talking about?"

His face went gray. "If you had touched me...or I had touched you..." He shook his head, going silent.

"What? What?" Maybe she didn't want to know.

"You would have become a Shade."

"A shade of what?"

"No, a Shade. A soulless, bodiless being."

"In other words, I'd be dead." Dying wasn't good. Not at all. Of course, since Azrael was a Reaper, she'd probably still get to be with him. And his existence didn't seem so bad.

"Yes, but—"

"We could spend more time together." The thought brighten the near death experience greatly.

"Not in the way you think." He stroked her cheek. "Shades have no contact, no communication, no comfort. They wander the Underworld, lost and alone. At best, you'd be able to see me. Maybe."

He sighed. "And one Shade is pretty much indistinguishable from the next. I'd have no way of knowing which one you were."

She shivered, and he pulled her close. "That's not going to happen, so don't even think of it." He touched his mouth to hers and she took some comfort in the brief kiss.

"Now," he said, "It's time to take you home."

* * *

Azrael watched Sara drive away, her kiss still warm on his lips. Amazing. A mortal woman had seen him in his visceral form and stood her ground. Even if she hadn't fully understood the consequences, it was impressive.

The ache in his heart was unfamiliar, but he recognized it anyway. Love. In one evening, he'd fallen for her completely. How could he not?

She knew who he was—what he was, and didn't shy away. She'd been at his side while he'd reaped souls and hadn't run. She was beautiful on the outside, yes, but the beauty within her was what drew him. He wanted her so badly he hurt.

Whatever it took, he would find a way to make her fall in love with him too.

He turned and walked into the alley where Pallidus waited, knowing full well the ridiculousness of his thoughts. No one could make a mortal do anything. They were creatures of free will.

Sara was not a woman who could be coerced. This evening had proven that.

A narrow grin lifted his mouth as he retook his Reaper form and mounted Pallidus for the journey home. She'd faced down his visceral form and given it no fear to feed on. She'd control the Darkness better than he'd ever been able to.

He sighed as Pallidus took to the skies. How would she react if he told her how he really felt? And what was the point? He couldn't offer her the kind of life a mortal woman expected.

Could he live half his time in the mortal world and half his time in his own and still fulfill his obligations as Reaper? He would have to find a way. No other option suited the situation. At least until...he shook his head. He would wait for her to cross over if that's what it took to be with her.

What if he told her the truth of his feelings and she wanted to join him sooner? He shuddered to think what she might do, as fierce as she was. When the time came, he would find a way to reap her soul himself, but not *until* her time came.

So for now, he would find a way to make this work. He would love her. He just wouldn't tell her.

Chapter Nine

The headache that woke Sara gave pain a new definition. She stumbled across the room to yank her shades down and block the light scraping her eyes like sandpaper.

The late night and red wine had cranked the vise at her temples tighter than ever. She downed some painkillers without water, then crawled back under the covers and tugged them over her to find total darkness. No run today. Maybe no shift at Grounded, either.

She curled up in a fetal position and tried to focus on more pleasant thoughts. Like Azrael's kiss. His hands. Dinner in Paris.

Headache or not, she smiled. How could she not? Last night had been unbelievable, even with the fact that she'd almost unknowingly done herself in.

Her fingers sought out the necklace he'd given her. She traced the curve of the wings, the tiny etched lines. Men didn't usually give jewelry casually.

Despite the pain in her head, she laughed softly. Did that mean the Angel of Death was her boyfriend? She was falling for him. Fast.

Good thing she was seeing him again tonight.

She groaned, remembering he was coming here. Why had she agreed to cook for him? That wasn't one of her best skills. She needed to figure out what to make, buy the ingredients, and clean the apartment.

None of that was going to happen with the kind of pain bouncing around in her skull at the moment. She'd be lucky if she made it in to the hospital. Groaning, she rose up on one elbow and reached for her day planner. She paged through to the day's date and checked her schedule.

Good. No shift at Grounded today. She shoved the book back onto her nightstand, pulled the covers back up and willed the headache away.

* * *

Sara peeked into her supervisor's office and knocked on the doorframe. "Brenda, you have a minute?"

"Sure, come on in." The older woman closed the file in front of her. "What can I do for you?"

"I was wondering...you know, I work a lot of hours, and I don't mind that, but...just for today, maybe I could leave early?"

"How early?"

"Four. Or four thirty. I won't take any lunch."

Brenda smiled. "You haven't taken time off in a long while, have you?"

"I took a half day last week when I cut my hand." She held up the fading scar.

"You're one of our most reliable employees. I think a half day now and then won't cause any irreparable damage." She wrote something down on a notepad. "Consider yourself off the clock at four."

Sara almost jogged back to the nurses' station. It would be close, but she should have all the time she needed to get her errands run. Provided her grocery list had something written on it. The dinner menu remained a mystery.

Steak was always a good bet, but the good stuff was expensive and she didn't own a grill. Fish? So many opportunities for that to go wrong. Pork? One letter away from porn and not all that romantic a meat to begin with. Lobster wasn't even close to affordable. Poultry was boring. Unless it was duck and you were eating at a sidewalk table in the most romantic city in the world. Maybe pasta. An old standby, but reliable and nearly foolproof.

And what if he was allergic? She laughed out loud. Chances were good "Angel of Death" and "food allergies" didn't usually end up in the same sentence.

"What's so funny?" Dane asked, tossing a paper cup in the trash. Dane was the only male nurse on the floor and the subject of many a batted eyelash. His surfer boy looks didn't make waves with her.

"Nothing, really." She sighed and tapped her pencil. "I'm trying to figure out a relatively easy meal that won't break my bank account. It also needs to have some seduction value."

"Seduction value?" He grinned. "What time should I be there?"

Dane dated anything with two X chromosomes. "Sorry, the position of dinner guest has already been filled."

He clutched his chest. "You're breaking my heart." He winked and leaned on the counter. "So who's the lucky guy? Somebody here?"

"No way. I'm done with doctors." She paused. How to explain Azrael. "He's just a nice guy."

"Nice?" Dane winced. "So this is your first and last date, then?"

"Why do you say that?"

"Nice is the kiss of death, every man knows that."

She bit her tongue to keep from laughing. Kiss of death indeed. She could go for some of that right now. "Okay, he's not that nice."

116

Shandra, another day shift nurse walked up. "Who's not that nice?"

Dane grinned. "Sara has a date."

"You do? With who?" Shandra asked.

Great. The entire hospital would know in about three minutes. "No one, just a guy."

"A *nice* guy," Dane added.

Shandra made sad eyes and clucked her tongue. "That's too bad."

"It's not too bad, and he's not a 'nice' guy. He could kill you just by looking at you," Sara growled.

Shandra and Dane exchanged a look and stepped back in unison.

"Well, not really. I don't think. Look, he's a great guy." Why she was getting upset, she didn't know. She didn't really care what they thought of him. Wasn't like they were ever going to meet him.

She raised her hands. "All right, calm down the two of you. I don't need every employee in this hospital thinking I'm dating a serial killer."

Dane arched a single brow. "So he's just killed the one time then?" His teasing tone relieved her. Crisis averted, it seemed.

"Oh no," she answered, keeping her voice light to hide the truth. "He's done in more people in than Jesse James."

"Ooo," Shandra cooed. "I love cowboys." She rested her forearms on the counter and leaned in. "You bringing him to the Halloween party?"

Dane elbowed Shandra. "That's a month away. She'll be dating me by then. Unless..." He wiggled his eyebrows at Shandra.

"Freak." Shandra pushed him away, laughing.

The top curve of a pair of wings appeared behind Shandra's shoulder. Sara went still, happy that Shandra and Dane were busy teasing each other.

Azrael leaned onto the counter, giving her a wink. She sat there, unmoving, unsure how to respond. If no one could see him but her, responding would make her look like she'd lost her marbles.

She gave him a weak smile. Shandra and Dane didn't notice it wasn't for them.

"Hi," Azrael said. "How are you? Last night was kind of a late night for you, wasn't it?"

"I'm fine," she whispered, burying her head in some paperwork.

He came around the counter and stood behind her, hands on her shoulders, and bent down so that his mouth was beside her ear. "I know you can't answer me. It's okay."

Her fingers went to the pendant around her neck. She nodded, whispered, "good."

"What?" Shandra asked.

"Nothing," Sara said.

Azrael kissed the side of her neck, making her inhale and scrunch up one shoulder. "I can't wait to see you tonight," he breathed against her skin.

On the other side of the counter, Dane and Shandra watched with interest.

"Don't you have work to do?" she asked. "Shoo!"

The pair went their separate ways, but their curious looks remained.

Azrael laughed and kissed her neck again. His mouth stayed dangerously close to her ear. "I'm here on business, but I couldn't resist seeing you." Then his mouth went lower on her neck. Heat radiated into her core. "Tonight cannot come fast enough."

She sighed and closed her eyes, too happy to wonder whose soul he'd come to reap. "This isn't fair," she said to the file in front of her, wondering if fanning herself with it would attract suspicion in the perpetually chilly building.

"Considering what I could be doing, you should be thankful." He breathed another kiss across her skin. "But I'll save that for later."

He left her shivering with need and anticipating the evening with a brand new set of nerves that stayed with her until she took off for the grocery store. Having something else to concentrate on helped. A little.

She wandered down the Italian foods aisle, amazed by the kinds of pasta beyond spaghetti. The idea of serving angel hair pasta made her smile. She added some fresh tomato sauce from the refrigerated section, a loaf of crusty bread, a bag of salad greens and a pint of her favorite ice cream, coffee chocolate chip. The only thing that tasted better was Azrael. Kissing him after a spoonful of that would probably push her right over the pleasure edge.

On her way home, she picked up two bottles of Chianti, then made a mental list of things to do as she finished the drive.

She hauled the groceries inside, unpacked and put them away, then surveyed her apartment. Nothing could be done about the less-than-pristine carpet. It had been that way when she moved in. The stupid strip of countertop had already come unglued, but she didn't have time to bother with that. How she longed for a home like the one she used to share with Ray. All that space. Everything new and perfect. But her salary would never cover a home like that.

At least this place was hers, and the rent let her tuck a few dollars into a vacation account each month. She smiled. Someday. The smile disappeared. If Ray paid his alimony like he was supposed to, someday would come a lot sooner.

She gave everything else a once over, vacuuming, polishing, dusting, straightening. Then she opened the sliding doors on her small balcony to let some fresh air in and the smell of cleaning products out.

Being home at this time of day was nice. She stood on the balcony overlooking a corner of the parking lot and let the sun warm her face. Another few weeks, it would be downright chilly, but today was a beautiful Indian summer day.

The trees flanking the small interior green space at the center of the apartment buildings already wore a pretty mix of oranges and yellows. A few leaves held on to their green, but not many.

Some kids threw a football around. Another neighbor walked his dog. She smiled at the small joys of life, and wondered why today seemed more perfect than words.

But in her heart, she suspected the reason would be knocking on her front door in about an hour. Her stomach knotted with anticipation.

Back inside, she set her small glass-topped table for two. There were no "best" dishes. Her everyday was the only set since the divorce. Her mother's china had gone to her brother, the bringer of grandchildren, and Ray's mother's china had stayed with Ray. Just as well. The delicate pink rose and green vine motif had never been her style.

"Bugger." She stood back and stared at the empty candleholders. She'd forgotten to get tapers. After some digging through various cabinets, she came up with a single white votive and a frosted glass cup. Yeah, that shouted romance. Blowing out a breath, she decided it would have to do.

She showered, shaved her legs—more a precautionary measure than a real plan—and rifled through her closet. Her wardrobe lacked a big selection of date clothes, but an embroidered white peasant blouse and jean skirt finally won out. Casual but sexy, especially with the blouse pulled down to expose her shoulders.

Hair, makeup, time to cook. Well, maybe not cook exactly, but she could get the bread ready and assemble the salad. The pasta would only take a few minutes.

Garlic bread would be the traditional way to go, but there would be kissing. There had better be. She was counting on it. Maybe just buttered and warmed would be okay. She sliced the bread, spread it with butter, then wrapped it in foil and popped it into the small oven.

Smiling, she set the temperature. She rarely cooked for herself. Fixing a meal for Azrael was so much better than cooking for one.

She emptied the container of sauce into a small pan set on low, then dug around for a decent bowl for the salad. Greens added, she sliced a tomato over them. Her mouth scrunched to one side. Greens and a single tomato made a rather pitiful salad.

Opening the cabinet that served as her panty, she stared hard, wishing better ingredients would magically materialize.

She pushed a few cans around. Hiding behind some chicken noodle soup was a small jar of marinated artichoke hearts. Part of the Italian food basket she'd won at a hospital charity raffle. She checked the expiration date. Hah! Years to go. Drained and mixed with the tomatoes, they jazzed up the salad.

Adding the bowl and a bottle of dressing to the small table left her with little else to do. What else could she do to occupy her time? Cheese. They needed grated cheese on the table.

Thirty seconds later, the task was complete and she was back to biting her lip and checking the time. Her heart beat twice as fast as the second hand of her watch.

She filled a stockpot with water and set it to boil for the pasta, adding a big dash of salt. He would be here soon. Maybe early. Of course, he hadn't been early to their first date. Seemed odd that Death would be lat—

A knock on her door made her jump. He was here. She choked back a squeal, then chastised herself for almost making such a desperate sound.

Act cool. She took a deep breath and checked her hair and lip-gloss in the hall mirror. Smiled. Too big. She scaled it back. Okay. That was better. More relaxed. Less desperate.

She opened the door, ready to greet her dinner guest. Her smile vanished and her stomach twisted hard. "What are you doing here?"

Chapter Ten

Ray shoved his way in. "You ought to know, you've got your lawyer hounding me."

Good to know her calls hadn't gone unheeded. She shut the door. The old panic rose like bile. "Just give me the check and get out."

His gaze traveled over her. "What are you all tarted up for? You going out?" He laughed. "Don't get me wrong, I'm all for it. The sooner you get remarried, the sooner I can stop writing alimony checks."

Ignore the jabs. Don't play into his game. She held her hand out. "Speaking of which."

He sniffed. "You're cooking?" Shaking his head, he walked down the hall and into her kitchen/living room/dining area. She chased after him. He lifted the lid off the saucepan. "You sure that's wise? Julia Child you're not."

"Same old Ray. Full of compliments." What had she ever seen in him beyond his looks and the M.D. after his name? "Do you have the alimony or not?"

He dipped his finger into the sauce, stuck it in his mouth and sucked it clean. "Not bad. Obviously from a jar, but you've managed to heat it up without burning it, so that's a start."

"I think it's time for you to leave." Check or not, his visit was over.

Leaning on the counter, he crossed his arms. "You look good. Lost that last five pounds, I see. Too bad you couldn't do that while we were married. I might have stuck around."

"Ten pounds actually and since you seem to have forgotten, I'm the one that left you, remember?" Idiot.

Another knock at the door interrupted him before he could answer. Her heart leapt. Some men had great timing. "You really should go now."

"And miss meeting your next ex-husband? Not a chance. Bring the sucker in." Ray narrowed his eyes at her and grinned, oblivious to what a smug jerk he was. Or maybe he enjoyed being an ass.

She turned on her heel, marched back to the entryway and opened the door. Azrael smiled from behind a huge bouquet of scarlet roses. Their delicate perfume wafted past her, erasing her nerves.

"These are for you." He handed the flowers to her. "I hope you like roses."

"I love them." She buried her nose in the velvet petals and inhaled again, only half-closing her eyes. Azrael looked so hot in jeans and a snug black sweater she couldn't take her eyes off him completely. Her inside went a little gooey. The man defined sexy. "They're beautiful. Thank you."

Holding the flowers to one side as he stepped in, she met him for a quick kiss on the mouth. "I'm really glad you're here," she whispered, unable to keep the tremor out of her voice or her gaze from angling back toward the kitchen.

He gave her a questioning glance, then looked down the hall. "What's wrong?" He kept his voice low.

"My ex-husband's here." She shook her head. "He owes me money, but he hasn't given it to me yet. He doesn't seem in any hurry to leave, either." She exhaled and dropped her head. What would Azrael think of her when he saw the kind of man she'd married? Would he understand she'd been young and foolish and completely mistaken?

Azrael lifted her chin with one hand and kissed her, giving her a wink. "I would be happy to assist you."

A new lightness bubbled up inside her. "Be my guest."

He started down the hall, then stopped. "I forgot to tell you. You look beautiful and dinner smells great." He resumed his march down the hall.

This should be good. She grinned as she followed him. Amazing what denim did for his backside. Or maybe it was what his backside did for denim. Either way, yum.

She walked into the kitchen behind Azrael and in time to see the startled look on Ray's face. What? Had he expected her to be dating some dweeb?

"Excuse me, I need to get a vase out of that cabinet for these beautiful roses." She dipped the bouquet toward the cabinet Ray stood in front of. He shuffled to the side without taking his eyes off Azrael.

"So you're the date?" Ray might have tried for snarky, but it came out too quiet.

"Not the date." Azrael folded his arms over his massive chest. "The boyfriend."

Too late to stop it, Sara giggled. Neither man looked at her. She ducked down, grabbed a vase from the cabinet and stuck it under the faucet to fill. Tendrils of steam escaped the lid on the pot of pasta water.

Azrael stood his ground in the center of the kitchen, narrowing the space even more. "You're the guy who couldn't keep her." It was a statement, not a question.

Heaven help her, she might actually be in love with him now.

Ray sputtered. "It wasn't that I couldn't, I mean it wasn't like I was the one who—"

"Whatever." Azrael moved to Sara's side and nudged his face against her neck. "Dinner smells great and so do you."

"Thanks." She giggled again. No one ever cut the great Dr. Whiteside off, especially not with such a flippant response.

Ray stood open-mouthed and silent. Sara thought he'd never looked so good. She cranked the faucet off and stuck the roses in the vase. She could recut the stems later. No way was she missing any of this.

If Azrael's eyes had been daggers, Ray would have been sliced stem to stern. "Why are you here?"

"He owes me alimony," she chimed in. Didn't look like Ray was capable of speech at the moment anyway.

Azrael nodded, slipping his arm around her waist. "Has he given it to you yet?"

"Nope."

Dropping his arm from her waist, Azrael took a step toward her ex.

A small, strangled sound leaked out of Ray. "I was just getting to that." He fumbled at his shirt pocket. "Here." He thrust the check at her.

She stuck it under a fridge magnet, next to a take-out menu and a coupon for tampons, which she quickly shoved under the menu.

"I'll see you out," Azrael said.

Ray took the long way out of the kitchen, around Azrael. "I can see myself out."

Azrael followed him. "I insist."

Sara stuck her head into the hall.

Ray hadn't gotten to the door fast enough. Azrael held it shut with one hand.

"Mail the checks from now on." The threat in Azrael's voice was unmistakable. "On time."

"Absolutely." Ray's Adam's apple bobbed like a plastic carnival duck.

Azrael stepped back. Ray snatched the handle and yanked the door open, disappearing in a blur.

"He didn't even say goodbye," Sara joked.

"Want me to get him back here?" Grinning, he shut the door and walked back to her.

"Not on your life." She shook her head. The man was amazing. "Hungry?"

"Yes." But the look in his eyes said not for food.

"Good, because I made enough for an army." Regardless of what either of them felt like doing, they were eating dinner first. "Thanks, by the way."

"For?" One brow slanted.

She tucked her forehead against his chest. "For...the roses." That wasn't what she'd meant at all.

He kissed the top of her head. "You're welcome."

Tipping her face toward his, she swallowed and found her courage. "What I really meant was thank you for...showing Ray that I was worth standing up for. And for telling him you're my boyfriend. That part was pretty cool. And completely unexpected."

"You're worth more than just standing up for. You're worth holding on to, and if that spineless cretin didn't understand that, then his loss and my gain." He brushed a strand of hair off her cheek, rubbing it between his fingers before letting it go. "I meant the boyfriend part. Unless that's assuming too much. Too fast."

"No, I'm okay with that." She giggled again, slapping a hand over her mouth. "Sorry, you seem to have an odd effect on me."

"It's mutual, believe me. I'm just not much of a giggler."

Strong arms tightened around her waist. She patted his chest. Hard as sun-baked clay and twice as hot. "I should fix dinner."

"Yes, you should." He dipped his head, found her mouth.

Her lips parted of their own volition, giving his questing tongue access. The gentleness of his kiss astounded her, but she felt no compunction to respond in like kind. Pulling back, she nipped his lower lip, then his jaw, working lower onto the thick column of his neck. His response came in long, low purring of her name.

"Sara..."

"Hmm?" she answered, too busy to form words. Her tongue traced swirls on his clean, slightly salty skin.

His arms crushed her tighter and evidence of his arousal pressed against her belly, fueling her own need. All he could do this time was moan.

Her hands snaked beneath his sweater. At the creamy heat of his skin beneath her hands, goose bumps peppered her arms. But the chill was temporary. His heat seared her fingertips, and like a moth drawn to flame, she wanted more.

The knowledge that he wanted her spurred her to boldness. She shoved his sweater up, splaying her fingers possessively on his body. She'd never been with a man like this. So much hard, hot muscle. Sure, Ray took care of himself, but Azrael was built for sin. She wanted to own him in the most wanton, animalistic way, but even more than that, she wanted him to own her back.

The hiss of water boiling over onto the stove's heating coil snapped her head up. She laughed to dissipate the heat spinning her head, and broke away, running to turn the burner down.

"I guess we should eat." She couldn't look at him, couldn't see the naked desire in his gaze. It would tug her back into his arms. And probably out of her clothes.

She dumped the box of angel hair into the boiling water. Truth was, the thought of sleeping with him split her down the middle. She wanted him more than anything, but she'd also been his first date, which probably meant she'd be his first—

He cleared his throat. "Definitely. You went to all this trouble, and no one's ever cooked for me before. I can't wait to try it."

That was exactly what she was talking about. Being someone's first usually meant you wouldn't be their last. She wasn't ready for him to realize how incredible sex was (at least she hoped that's what he'd think), then go chase after it with every willing woman. She glanced over her shoulder. He flashed a smile that would bring sight to a blind woman's eyes. Who wouldn't be willing?

She shrugged. "It was no trouble, really."

"You cook like this all the time then?" He settled into her one and only barstool, crossing his arms on the counter. Someday the matching stool would show up at the Goodwill.

"Not hardly. I work too much." She stirred the pasta to keep it from sticking, then readied the colander in the sink. "I should cook more often, but it's hard to cook for one. I make too much and get sick of eating it, you know?"

He shook his head. "Not really. I don't cook."

"At all?" She turned. "Or do you not need to eat?"

"No, I eat. Not much, but I do. I have...help with the cooking."

Images of undead French maids filled her head. Maybe they had wings too. Great. The French maids morphed into leggy Victoria's Secret supermodel sashaying through Azrael's underworld kitchen in their angel outfits, great steaming platters of gourmet cuisine in hand. "What kind of help?"

"Staff."

The pasta was probably done. "And that means?"

He laughed. "There's nothing to be jealous of, I assure you. They are merely former Shades given enough life to be functional."

"I'm not jealous." She was totally jealous. "Just curious." She slipped on oven mitts and grabbed the pasta pot. Steam fogged her vision as she drained the angel hair. "I thought Shades were sort of, nonentities."

"They are. But the Fates have turned a few into servants for Chronos and me."

"What about Mr. Death Eyes?" She pitied anyone, dead or otherwise, who had to spend time with Kol.

"He has to fend for himself."

134

She laughed short and sharp. "Seems fair." She slid the pasta back into the pot, added the warmed sauce, then gave the whole thing a good stir.

"Kol's not really as bad as you think. Just..." Azrael's mouth twisted to one side.

"I know. He's your brother. I shouldn't have said anything." She forked pasta onto plates. "I have a brother too. He's older by almost ten years. We live completely different lives in completely different cities. We talk maybe once a year, exchange a card or two, but other than that, there's no interaction. Still, he's my brother. I wouldn't want anyone talking bad about him either."

He looked relieved. "There is no excuse for Kol so I won't try to make one. But he lives a much different existence than Chronos and I. Much lonelier."

"Yeah, well, he didn't strike me as the warm, cuddly type so I can understand." She sighed. "Sorry again."

"It's okay." He leaned back. "What about the rest of your family?"

"My dad died my senior year of high school. Nearly destroyed my mother. My brother'd been married four years by then and had twins on the way, so when I left for college, she moved to Seattle to be close to him, help with the babies." She shrugged. "She thinks I should have tried to make things work with Ray."

He snorted. "I disagree."

"See? That's why I like you." She picked up the plates and headed for the table. Stopping halfway, she turned to face him. "Are you lonely?"

The look on his face said the question had caught him off guard. "Not so much anymore." His lop-sided smile made her inside tumble. "Anything I can do to help?"

She was falling. Hard. She stared at the plates, hoping he hadn't seen anything telling in her eyes. She didn't want to scare him away. "Do you know how to open a bottle of wine?" She pointed with her elbow to the bottle of Chianti on the table. "There's an opener beside the bottle."

"I think I can figure that out." He rose and went to the table to inspect the bottle she'd indicated.

While he worked on the cork, she put the plates on the table, then got the bread out of the oven and tucked the slices into a napkin-lined basket.

As she brought it to the table, he put the bottle down and pulled out her chair, waited for her to sit, then returned to his task. Victory followed soon after with a resounding pop. He poured for them both, then sat across from her.

"This looks great." He lifted his gaze from the plate. "Angel hair, right?"

She grinned. "Yeah, I was being funny."

Smiling, he stabbed his fork into the strands of pasta and lifted a slice of gray out of the sauce. "This isn't a Death Angel mushroom then, is it?"

"No." She laughed. "I didn't even know there was such a thing." She crossed her heart. "Promise." She twirled pasta around her fork. "What kind of stuff do you usually eat?"

"Nothing much, really. I need very little food unless I'm in human form."

"That explains why there's not an ounce of fat on you." She took a bite and was pleasantly surprised with her efforts.

"Maybe if you were in my kitchen, I'd feel differently." He tore off a slice of bread and bit into it, chewing with gusto.

She laughed. "This is about as basic a meal as you get, I'm sure your staff could manage this."

"My staff doesn't affect me the way you do."

She sipped her wine, willing it to either cool the heat rushing through her or tame her tongue. It did neither.

She set her glass down and met his hungry gaze. "And what way would that be?"

Chapter Eleven

The tiniest smudge of sauce clung to the corner of Sara's mouth. He'd never wanted a taste of something more in his life. How could he explain to her the way she made him feel without scaring her away? Mortals found their way through their emotions much slower. He'd already thought this through. This wasn't the right time to speak his heart, no matter how much he wanted to tell her.

Maybe he should tell her that he'd nearly reaped her ex-husband's soul. The desire to punish the man still rippled in his gut. The control it had taken to keep the Darkness at bay...he wouldn't think of that now. Sara waited for an answer.

"You make me...hot."

She laughed, a sound he thought he never grow tired of. "Hot?"

That hadn't been the right word. "You make me...want you."

This time she blushed the shade of the wine in her hand. She canted her head, hiding her eyes.

Not what he'd been going for either. He didn't want her to think he was only after one thing. He wasn't Chronos or Kol. "I like you, Sara. I'm just not good at expressing myself." A lie, but one that bought him time.

"I think you're very good at expressing yourself." She spoke quietly without looking at him.

"I didn't mean to embarrass you, and I didn't mean that the only affect you have on me is physical. It isn't. I'm just not ready to express everything I feel yet." He couldn't get any plainer than that.

Her chin rose, but her color hadn't changed. "See? You did fine." The disappointment in her voice was unmistakable.

He reached across the table and took her hand. "I can't imagine myself with another woman, Sara. I mean that. I think about you when I'm not with you. I wonder what you're doing. If other men...mortal men..."

"No." She shook her head. "I'm not interested in anyone else."

"I wanted to hurt Ray." What had made him blurt that out, he didn't know.

She laughed hard, tugging her hand away to cover her mouth. "I wanted you to, too," she managed between gasps. Tears leaked from the corners of her eyes and she struggled to catch a breath. "Oh, that's awful, but it's true. He's such a pompous jerk."

She wiped her eyes and lifted her wine in toast. "You were so good with him. Put him in his place in a way I've never seen anyone do."

"You don't have to take his money if you don't want to." Any association with her ex-husband was a bad one as far as Azrael was concerned. He wanted to be the one taking care of her, the one she could rely on.

She sighed. "Actually I do. I'm in the hole from the divorce. The lawyer wasn't cheap. I know this place doesn't look like much, but at this point it's all I can afford."

"You deserve better." Much better.

"I appreciate that, I really do—"

"I can give you better."

Her mouth opened but no sound came out. She closed it, then finally spoke. "Do you mean what I think..."

"I'll buy you a place, anywhere you want."

"You do mean what I think you mean." She straightened her silverware on the napkin. "That's very sweet, but I couldn't possibly do something like that."

"Why not?" If he was in Reaper form, he could have used the power of his gaze to persuade her. Both he and Chronos possessed a tiny bit of Kol's power—not enough

140

to reap souls—that was Kol's curse alone. But he didn't want her to acquiesce like that. He wanted it to be her true decision.

Her fingers lingered on the knife handle. "I hardly know you."

Had he used the word boyfriend too soon? He thought her eyes had sparkled when he'd said it. Perhaps he'd been mistaken. "You've seen a side of me only my brothers have ever seen. How much more do you want to know?"

Her hands fell back into her lap. "This place is fine, really."

"Sara, what are you afraid of?"

"Nothing."

"Liar." He kept his tone light, hoping she'd tell him what she was really feeling, even if she made a joke of it. "Tell me."

She sipped her wine, stayed silent a few moments longer than was comfortable. "That you'll...figure things out and leave."

He narrowed his eyes. "Figure things out?"

"You said I was your first date, right? Well, I know men. I won't be your last. You'll sleep with me and figure out how much you like sex and then you'll be gone, chasing after the next conquest, and where will I be? Long forgotten, that's where." She pressed her fingers to

141

her mouth, looking slightly mortified. "I think I've had enough wine."

Sitting back in his chair, he did his best not to grin. She'd been thinking about them sleeping together. Good to know they were of like minds on that. "You might know men, I'll give you that. But would you agree I'm not your ordinary man?"

"Yes." She wasn't looking at him, but she was answering. A good sign.

"And if I had invested in this relationship by purchasing a safer home for you—a place completely your own, with your name alone on the deed—don't you think that would be a substantial bit of incentive for me to stick around?"

"Probably." She slanted her eyes at him, just for a moment. "But that doesn't change the fact that you could have any woman you wanted."

"You think most women would want to date a Reaper?"

Her eyes met his. "In your human form, they wouldn't know the difference."

"But I would." He leaned forward. "And I already have the woman I want."

"I don't know. I don't know." She pushed away from the table and walked into the kitchen.

He went after her. "It wasn't my intention to upset you."

"You didn't. And it's a very generous offer, but—"

He held his hand up. "Think about it, that's all I ask."

She nodded, exhaling a soft breath. "Okay. Fair enough."

Taking her hands, he pulled her back toward the table. "Come eat or I'll feel like I ruined the evening."

A slight smile teased her lush mouth and she came willingly. "You didn't ruin it."

They sat back down and ate, keeping the conversation to safe subjects like the family she never saw and her job.

"I can't eat any more or I'll explode. How do mortals do this, always feeling so full?" He pushed his plate away.

She grinned. "We don't always eat until we feel sick. You'll have to learn to pace yourself."

"When it tastes good, it's hard to stop."

She picked up the plates and carried them into the kitchen. "I hope you saved room for dessert. It's my favorite ice cream. If you don't like it, I won't be able to date you anymore."

He stiffened in his chair.

Her laughter rang out. "I'm just teasing. Something like that isn't going to stop me from seeing you."

Dishes clattered under running water. Azrael picked up the breadbasket and salad bowl and carried them in.

"Thanks," she said, "but I'll clean up. Go sit. You're the guest."

"As you wish." He relaxed on the sofa. She joined him with two bowls a few minutes later.

"Here. Coffee chocolate chip. Prepare to know the meaning of the word bliss." She dug into hers without waiting. Her eyes closed and a soft *mmmm* slipped from her closed mouth.

Scoops of chocolate-speckled tan ice cream filled the chilly bowl. He doubted anything could taste better than kissing her, but he'd try it to make her happy. The ice cream melted on his tongue, mingling the earthiness of the coffee with the bittersweetness of the chocolate.

It was good. But he could think of a way to make it better. He put his bowl down on the small table in front of the sofa and reached for her.

"What are you doing?" She held her ice cream up, laughing. "You have your own bowl."

"I don't want your ice cream. I want you. I want to taste it on you." His hands found her waist and tugged her close. With her bowl still up over her head, his mouth met hers. He swept his tongue past the seam of her lips to tangle with hers, coffee-flavored and cold from the sweet treat. He warmed it up quickly.

She pulled away long enough to set her bowl beside his. "You're a naughty boy. I'm trying to eat my ice cream."

"You'd rather have the ice cream?" Before she could answer, he yanked his sweater over his head.

Her eyes widened and she inhaled, mouthing a silent *wow*.

Taking that as a good sign, he dipped his finger into the puddle of melted ice cream in his bowl, then trailed it down his chest.

She whimpered softly, a needy, hungry sound. "You have the devil in you."

He beckoned with his finger. "Maybe you can teach me to behave."

"I doubt it." Pushing onto her knees, she scooted toward him. "But I'm willing to try."

She bent her head to the line of ice cream and cleaned it off his chest with a single pass of her silky tongue. The sensation sucked the breath from his lungs. She sat back with a satisfied grin and surveyed her work. "I've never seen a body like yours in person."

"And?" It almost embarrassed him how badly he needed to know her opinion of him.

She flattened her palms on his chest, splaying her fingers against his skin. His body tightened, honing his nerves to focus on the points of contact. Her scent enveloped him. He was her servant at that moment, lost to any existence but pleasing her.

"And..." A coy smile, at odds with her actions, lit her beautiful face. "I like it. Very much. Like touching it. All that hard muscle and soft, warm skin."

Straddling his body, she settled into his lap. His hands rested loosely on her hips in hopes she wouldn't notice his trembling. What was greater than want? More powerful than need? Whatever it was, he felt it.

"Am I in any danger of unleashing that other side of you?" she asked, pushing him back onto the sofa.

"No." Desire thickened his words. "Not while I'm in human form."

"Good." She picked up one of the ice cream bowls and tipped it, drizzling a line of cream down his stomach. The cold liquid did nothing to cool his feverish skin. Her mouth followed, licking and nibbling at the sticky sweetness. If she couldn't feel what she was doing to him, she must be numb from the neck down.

He couldn't take it anymore. He grabbed her shoulders and pulled her up, sliding her over the remaining slick of melted ice cream.

"Hey, my blouse—"

"I'll buy you a new one." The time for words was over. He crushed her mouth with a savage kiss. One hand griped the back of her neck, buried beneath the silk of her hair. The other found the small of her back and pressed her hips into his. There should be no question in her mind as to what effect she had on him now.

She groaned low in her throat. Her body rocked against his hard length. He trailed kisses down the column of her neck, causing her to moan again.

"I don't know if I'm ready for this..." she whispered, her breath coming in long draws.

"I won't leave you," he breathed against her raspberry-scent skin. "I give you my word. I'll take care of everything. You'll never want for anything ever again, my sweet Sara."

She stiffened in his arms. Pulled away. "I didn't agree to anything. I don't need to be taken care of."

"You don't?"

"No."

The firmness of her tone cooled his body where her warm length had been pressed. Desire, need, hunger...it surged, looking for a way out. A release. But there would be none. She didn't want him the way he wanted her. Humiliation took control of his tongue. "Look around. I could offer you so much more than this."

He stood, thankful the result of their heated actions had already begun to recede. "I don't know what's wrong with wanting to take care of you. With wanting to make your life better."

"My life is fine." She shook her head, eyes bright. "I won't be controlled by another man. I won't."

"I don't want to control you." If all mortal women responded to sincere gestures like this, he could better understand why his brothers didn't get involved. "I want to take care of you."

"I don't need to be taken care of." Her mouth thinned to a fine line. "Not by you or anybody else."

"You didn't mind my help with your ex-husband."

She pulled her knees up, wrapped her arms around them. "Maybe you should go."

He spread his arms. "Sara, please. Why can't you understand what I'm trying to do?" How had this gone so wrong?

"I understand perfectly. That's why I got divorced in the first place."

"I'm nothing like him. Nothing." His insides shattered. He didn't care if he had to plead. He needed her. This stubborn, beautiful woman couldn't see she already owned his heart.

She shook her head and spoke without looking at him. "Maybe you aren't, but that's a chance I'm not willing to take."

Chapter Twelve

"There are no threads," Atropos said, holding her empty hands up for him to see.

Azrael wanted to curse the old woman's tricks, but kept his tongue. In a week's time, there'd been far too few souls to reap lately. For him anyway. Kol and Chronos had been busy enough they'd had little time to speak with him. And so he'd spent nearly every moment missing Sara. Wanting to talk to her, but not knowing what to say. Wanting to explain, but not knowing how.

She'd told him to leave. He doubted she would welcome him back. Stubborn, thickheaded, beautiful woman.

"Then cut some," he growled. "There must be need." He glared at Klotho and Lachesis. They quickly bowed their heads back to their work.

"There isn't." Atropos polished her shears with a scrap of silk. She admired her reflection in their brilliant finish. "If you miss her, go to her."

"It isn't that simple." He paced the limestone balcony. All the sweet-scented breezes and trickling water in the world couldn't soothe him today.

"Of course it is," she countered. "That is the way of love."

He whipped back, care for his behavior gone. "What would you know of love, old woman?"

Her cackle bit into his skin. "I know that you are in it."

Klotho covered her mouth too late to hide her smile and Lachesis's laugh sharpened into a cough.

He stared at the pair. "It comforts me to know you find such amusement in the chaos you've helped create."

Lachesis returned his gaze, wide-eyed and full of surprise. "That we've helped create?" She clucked her tongue. "No one put words in your mouth or feelings in your heart. You did that yourself."

"Poor Azrael," Klotho cooed. "You should go to her. Offer her a gift...mortal women love gifts."

His scowl erased her smile. "Not this one."

"Does she still wear your amulet?" Klotho asked.

"How would I know?" He exhaled hard. "I haven't seen her in a week."

Klotho shrugged and went back to her spinning. "If it still hangs about her neck, I would think that a good sign."

"A very good sign," Lachesis interrupted. "You should visit her. See for yourself."

"No. Not without reason." He wouldn't crawl to her like some lovesick boy. Not unless he had to. Which he might.

Lachesis beckoned to Atropos. "Come look at this thread." She held one against her staff, tipping her head in study.

Atropos made her way over. She tipped her head as well, tapping a gnarled finger on her whiskered chin. "Hmm. You have a good eye, Lachesis."

She pulled her shears free of their pouch, snipped the thread, then turned to dangle it in his direction.

"Here." She held it out. "Go."

* * *

Stupid.

Sara slammed the file drawer shut. She'd been stupid. Hung up on her past. All because that idiot Ray had rattled her cage. It wasn't possible to hate anyone more than she hated him. Although she wasn't very happy with herself at the moment.

An entire week had gone by without even the briefest glimpse of Azrael at the hospital. She hadn't expected a phone call or email, but the way he'd disappeared...or maybe he had been there and she could no longer see him. The thought tightened her throat, brought heat to her eyes. She clutched the silver wings at the hollow of her throat. Holding that reminder of him soothed her a little.

Worst of all, she had no way to contact him. No way to apologize or make him understand about her past and the way Ray had warped her mind.

Where are you, Azrael? Just show up and I'll apologize until I'm blue.

The man had offered to buy her a place to live, no strings attached, and she'd told him to get out. What woman in her right mind turned down an offer like that from a guy whose kisses made her see fireworks? And even if there had been strings, she'd been ready to sleep with him that night. What other strings could there be?

She threw the files down and slumped into the desk chair. There had to be a way to find him or get a message to him. Something. Anything. Sighing, she propped her elbows on the desk and leaned her forehead on the heels of her palms. Think, think, think.

Maybe Azrael was avoiding her, but that didn't mean his brothers were. She rested her chin on her fists. She needed to find someone right as they were about to die. As morbid as that was, it might be her only chance.

This was a hospital, how hard to could that be? Her first thought was the morgue, but at that point, it was already too late. She bounced her thumbs off her jaw. Where...to...go.

She sat up. Twisted around.

"Dane. Hey. Dane."

He looked up from a chart. "Yeah? What's the emergency?"

She grinned, jumped out of her chair. "Exactly. Taking a break. Back in a few."

"Hey, you can't..."

But she was halfway down the hall.

Busy described the emergency room, but there were many words that worked better. Chaotic. Noisy. Scary. A person didn't end up here because they were in perfect working order. This was exactly where she needed to be. She scanned the crowded waiting room. Nothing.

The hospital badge hanging from the lanyard around her neck made her invisible to the staff bustling from one area to another. She slipped through the doors beyond the waiting room with some medical personal.

Here the beds were portioned off with curtains only, no walls like the rooms up stairs. This was serious business. There was no time for true privacy when lives were on the line.

She shuffled past the thin, drawn curtains, listening, trying to catch a peek between the joins of fabric. A nurse rushed past, yelling commands for medication Sara didn't completely understand, but the woman's tone conveyed enough meaning.

Someone was in critical condition.

Sara headed in the direction the nurse had come from, toward the next room of beds. She rounded the doorway and stopped cold as fear sucked the breath from her lungs.

Kol from a distance was nothing compared to Kol less than ten feet away.

Tight-lipped, he leaned against the wall near the bed of a twenty-something man, a gang-banger if the street-style tattoos and shaved head meant anything. Doctors and nurses worked frantically to keep the man from bleeding out from a gunshot wound.

Sara stepped back thinking Kol had come toward her, but then she realized it was his voluminous black leather coat moving of its own volition, shifting subtlety like the coils of a snake.

His lanky black hair swept his collar and trailed past his shoulders. At his temple swung a single braid knotted through a small bead that looked very much like a knucklebone.

As tall as Azrael, he was less broad, more sinewy. Where Azrael was sculpted, Kol was angles. Everything about him looked hard, angry. Ready to fight. A junkyard dog that'd gone too many days without a meal.

Sara shivered. This was a bad idea. She retreated, hoping the eyes behind those dark glasses were focused on the dying man.

Kol's head lifted half an inch.

"Come to see how the other third lives, sweetheart?"

In his derisive tone, the term of endearment sounded more like a curse. Her feet froze to the floor. She shook her head, swallowed hard.

"Am...am I the only one who sees you?" she whispered.

"Do you see anybody freaking out? Mortals only see me when I want them to. Except for you."

"Oh. Good." She kept her voice down. Not that anyone would really notice her talking to herself in the chaos of the ER.

"Yeah, it's freaking fabulous." Kol crossed his arms, the seams of his coat weeping what looked like tears.

"I was...wondering...if you knew where—"

His gaze still aimed at the soul to be reaped, he lifted a finger and pointed to the expiring man. "Meth dealer. Two weeks of nightmares. Nothing." He shrugged. "Idiot mortal."

She had no clue what Kol was talking about, but as long as he wasn't focused on her, she was okay. Scared witless, but okay.

"Favorite haunt was North Franklin Middle School." He turned his head in her direction. Thankfully, the glasses stayed put. He shook his head slowly. "Can't have that, now can we?"

Her tongue stuck to the roof of her mouth. "N-no," she whispered.

"We're losing him," one of the doctors called out.

"Be right with you, dollface. Little matter to take care of first." He peeled off the wall with the soft, sticky sound of damp leather being stripped from heavily painted concrete block and walked toward the bed. Halfway, he paused and glanced over his shoulder. "You might not want to watch this. Or whatever."

She didn't want to watch, especially after being warned, but she couldn't look away. And since her vantage point didn't give her a straight on view of his eyes, she felt like she'd be safe. Mostly.

Kol spread his arms. His coat billowed into black wings. He had no scythe this time, something Sara didn't know if she should be grateful for or not.

As Kol approached the bed the man began to moan. If the doctors and nurses heard it, they didn't react. Kol went closer and the moans rose into terrified shrieks.

"More plasma, stat! We need an OR now!" The medical team kept working, struggling to save a life, oblivious to the scene playing out in front of them.

156

Kol hovered at the head of the bed. He ripped his shades off. "Your time is up, dirtbag."

Fathomless black holes stared into the dying man. The shriek became one long keening wail that pierced her head and made her joints ache. Black ooze flowed out of the man. Sara shut her eyes, unable to watch any further.

The sound disappeared. She opened her eyes. The medical staff was at rest, no longer trying to save the man.

"Call it." One of the doctors checked his watch and pronounced the death. Kol had disappeared.

"Looking to come to the dark side?"

She jumped and spun around. He wasn't gone, he was right behind her. Fortunately, his shades were in place. "You scared the crap out of me."

"Another job well done." He grinned. "And yes, I'm free tonight if that answers your question." He tipped his head. "But only one night. You're cute, but I bore easily."

Pig. She ignored him. "Do they always scream like that?" She snuck a peek at the man whose soul Kol had just reaped. A nurse prepped the body for the morgue.

"You heard that?" Kol stood a little straighter, his brows drawing together in question.

"Yes. It was awful."

"Do you still hear it?" He leaned closer.

She pulled back. "No. Does that mean you do?"

157

His curious expression morphed into a hard mask of anger and disgust. He looked away, putting an end to her questions. "What do you want? I have work to do."

"I need to get a message to Azrael."

Kol's head swiveled back in her direction. He licked his finger and held it up, testing some non-existent wind.

"Looks like you're in luck, sweetcheeks."

* * *

Little noise disturbed the peace of the cancer ward. A few nurses talking, the sound of a cart being wheeled through the hall. Not much else. The thread in Azrael's pocket would be a small ripple in the pond, enough to clear the nurse's station.

And he could find Sara. Talk to her. Smooth things. He hoped.

The soul in need belonged to a middle-aged man suffering from lymphoma. Azrael slipped into the man's room, released his soul and returned to the hall. Within minutes a nurse came to the room.

He made his way toward the desk. Would Sara smile when she saw him? Frown? Ignore him? What if she couldn't see him anymore? No. He wouldn't think about that possibility.

Rounding the corner brought him up short. She wasn't there. He checked the visitor's room. Not there either, so he went back and waited near the desk. Minutes ticked by. Still no Sara.

Since no one could see him, including the male nurse sitting where Sara usually sat, Azrael went behind the desk and into the office to look for a schedule. As best as he could tell, she was supposed to be here.

He had no choice but to change forms. An unlocked supply closet served to give him privacy. Wouldn't do to have some one see him appear in the middle of the hall. Putting his ear to the door, he listened for footsteps, heard nothing. Satisfied with the quiet, he opened the door a crack and checked the hall. No one.

He looked in both directions before slipping out. All clear. Adopting a confident air, he strode back to the desk. The male nurse glanced up as Azrael approached.

"Can you help me? I'm looking for someone." Azrael kept a friendly smile on his face.

The nurse—Dane according to his hospital badge—shook his head. "Visiting hours are over. I don't know how you got up here, but you're going to have to leave."

"I'm not here to see a patient. The woman I'm looking for works here. Sara Donovan?"

Dane leaned back and crossed his arms. "What do you need to see her about?"

"It's personal," Azrael answered, hoping his tone shut the door on that line of questioning.

Dane cracked a know-it-all grin. "You the guy she's been moping about all week?"

"She's been moping?" That was a good sign.

"Yeah. Been a real bear to work with, too." Dane leaned forward. "Look, it's none of my business but—"

"You're right. It isn't any of your business, so stay out of it."

Azrael and Dane turned simultaneously in the direction of the interrupter.

Hands on her hips, Sara stood in the hallway. Kol stood right behind her, waggling his brows suggestively, but Azrael only had eyes for Sara.

She jabbed a finger in his direction. "We need to talk."

Chapter Thirteen

Dean rolled his eyes. "Great. I take it that means you're still on break?"

"Yes. Suck it up," Sara said.

Kol snickered. "You said suck."

Ugh. As Reapers went, Kol was her least favorite. The sooner he went on his merry way the better.

Dane looked back at Azrael, clearly oblivious to Kol. "See, I told you. She's been like this all week."

Azrael didn't take his eyes off her. Leaving Dane behind, he went to her. "Sara...I—"

She held her hands up. "We need to talk in private." Keeping her hand in front of her, she jerked her thumb toward Kol.

Azrael looked over her shoulder. "Leave, Kol."

"And miss all the fun?" Kol miffed.

"Go," Azrael commanded.

"I have better things to do anyway."

Sara heard a soft whoosh, like a match being lit. "Is he gone?"

"Yes."

"Good. Let's go to the visitor's room." She held her hand out to Azrael. To her relief, he took it.

"I hope you two lovebirds work things out," Dane called down the hall after them. Sara ignored him. Patients were trying to sleep, after all.

Once in the visitor's room, she shut the door. She didn't bother with the lights.

"Azrael, I—"

"Sara, I—"

They both spoke at once, stopped and smiled.

"Ladies first," Azrael said.

"Good, because I was the one in the wrong," Sara said.

"No," Azrael countered. "I never should have pushed my will on you that way."

"I know you had my best interests at heart. I just have a past that makes moving forward hard for me sometimes."

He stepped closer. "I would never treat you like that, Sara."

She nodded, dropping her head a bit. "I know."

"You should also know my feelings for you..."

She looked up. He'd turned away and now stared at the floor. Whatever he needed to tell her, she would understand. If his feelings had changed because of what had happened, she would work to rebuild things between them. If he was willing. "You can tell me. Whatever it is. I don't want you to feel like you have to hide anything from me."

"I don't know." He shook his head. "I don't want to frighten you."

"Kol hit on me. I think my 'frighten' threshold is pretty high." She smiled, but immediately saw the look in Azrael's eyes was anything but amused.

"He hit on you?" He stepped toward the door. "That son of a—"

"Whoa." She caught him with her hands on his chest. "It was nothing, really. I get the sense he would have laid the same lines on Pallidus."

That sent a small grin to Azrael's full mouth. "Pallidus would have kicked him."

"How do you know I didn't?"

He laughed, slipped his hands around her waist. "Because you're still alive." He bent his head to nuzzle her cheek. "I've missed you terribly."

Her hands slid up his chest until she interlaced her fingers behind his neck. "I've missed you too. I'm really sorry about everything—"

"Let's forget it. Move on. Can we? I don't want to spend my time with you being sorry for what's in the past."

She nodded. Not rehashing her mistakes was fine with her. "What was it you were going to say to me earlier?"

"I think it's best left unsaid. At least for now."

"Please." She needed to know. Was dying to know.

He inhaled deeply, his chest expanding against hers. "Sara...I can't say with absolute certainty as I've never had these feelings before, and certainly never for a mortal, you must understand that, but I believe—"

"You ramble a bit when you're nervous, you know that?" She winked. "Just spit it out."

He swallowed. "I love you."

Her knees buckled, but he caught her.

"Oh." He loved her. Loved. Her. "I need to sit."

He swept her into his arms, picking her up without effort. "How's this?"

She couldn't answer him. Couldn't look at him. Not yet. Not before she tried to make sense of what he'd said. This man...this being...loved her. Did she love him back? That wasn't the right question. Could she love him back? What were the consequences of loving him? Did she care when being in his arms felt this good?

She glanced up. "Are you sure about this?"

164

"As much as I can be. I've had no experience—"

"What does your heart tell you?"

"That it cannot bear to be without you." The sincerity in his gaze nearly brought tears to her eyes.

She didn't want to hurt him. He might be Death incarnate but he was, by his own admission, also a man. The male ego could be a fragile thing. She cupped his cheek. "I...I need a little more time. To get to know you more...as a person."

His mouth thinned, but he nodded. "Whatever time you need. But please, one thing."

"Sure."

His lids shuttered down, hiding his eyes. "I find I am a jealous man."

She smiled. "You don't want me to see anyone else?"

"Maybe it's not fair of me to ask..."

Her thumb grazed his cheekbone. "I won't be seeing anyone else, believe me."

Their gazes met. "Thank you," he whispered, sealing his words with a kiss of gratitude.

She kissed him back, hungry for the mouth that turned her spine to butter, but aware of their surroundings. When her control thinned to the point that the idea of getting him naked in the visitor's room seemed rational, she broke the kiss. "I think I can stand on my own now."

"I don't want to put you down." He nibbled the edge of her lips.

She sighed, wishing they were somewhere else. "Wouldn't be my choice either, but I'm still on the clock."

He eased her to her feet. "I must see you soon, Sara."

"I know the feeling." She clung to him, not ready to return to work.

"When will you be done this evening?"

She shook her head. "I can't tonight. I'm exhausted and I have a shift at Grounded tomorrow morning."

He growled softly and clenched his fists. "You don't need that other job. I could—"

She put her hands on her hips. "We just went through this, didn't we?"

"I don't care. I want to spend time with you."

The little boy neediness coming out of him was cute, but she did her best not to smile. "I need to pay my bills on my own. You're just going to have to understand that."

"Fine." Except the look on his face said he wasn't. "When do you work?"

"I'm on eight to one at Grounded, then here three to eleven. We could meet for lunch, if you want."

"I want more than lunch, but I'll take what I can get." He crossed his arms, petulant as all get out.

She gave him a smile. "Thank you for understanding." She went up on her tippy-toes to peck his cheek. "I'll meet you at Little Mac's, the deli across from the parking garage, around 1:15 okay?"

He grunted something that sounded affirmative. She tried not to laugh. The Angel of Death had the hots for her.

Of all the men in all the world, she got the one that, well, wasn't.

* * *

"Mmm, mmm, mmm." Keysha poked Sara in the ribs. "Check out that fine slice in the club chair by the mug display. Makes your drawers damp, don't he? Not that he's taken his eyes off you long enough to notice a fine sister like myself."

Sara wiped her arm across her forehead and looked up from the espresso machine. How many had she made today? A hundred? A hundred and fifty? She followed Keysha's gaze.

And froze. He made her drawers damp all right. Azrael lifted his cup of coffee in salute.

A hot tickle snaked up her spine. She turned away, brushed the loose tendrils of hair back into her ponytail. "How long has he been here?"

"Since right after the morning rush. You know him?"

"He's my lunch date." She bit her lip to keep from grinning. "And sort of my boyfriend."

"Sort of? You mean you don't know for sure? You want me go ask him?" Keysha laughed.

"No," Sara shook her head, eyes wide. Keysha would do it, too. "I already know what he'd say. I'm still trying to figure things out."

"Well don't wait too long. A man like that won't hang around forever."

"Not him. He's different."

"Different? Don't tell me the brother's out of work? Is that why he's here? You're not giving him money, are you?"

"Shh. No, it's nothing like that. He's got plenty of money." Her fingers went to the pendant at her neck. "He gave me this on our first date."

"All right, that's cool." Keysha peered at the necklace, then back at Azrael. "He got any brothers?"

"Yes, but trust me, they're nothing like him."

"No big." Keysha shrugged. "Least one of us is getting a little something."

Sara felt her face heat. "We're not exactly there yet."

Keysha rolled her eyes. "Fine looking white boy like that and you're sitting on your hands. Damn shame, you ask me." She pressed against the front counter, called out the name for the next order to be picked up, then came back to lean against the wall by Sara. "He your first since the divorce?"

168

"Yes. And I'm..."

"Nervous?"

"A little." How could she explain that Azrael was the Angel of Death *and* a virgin, and her worries about sleeping with him went way beyond nerves?

Keysha waved her hand. "They say it's like riding a bike, but it's not even that hard. Just let it happen, you know? Let nature take its course." She smiled. "You work too hard not to let loose once in a while. And seriously, that man over there is like a major opportunity to get buck freakin' wild."

Laughter bubbled up out of Sara. "That he is." She snuck a glance in his direction. Sunlight streaming in from the window behind him outlined him with a warm glow. His faded jeans, gray tee and black leather jacket accentuated his athletic build. He winked. Gorgeous didn't do him justice.

"Take five minutes." Keysha nudged her away from the espresso machine. "Go say hi. I'll finish cleaning this beast."

"You sure?"

"I'm the manager, aren't I?" She slanted her eyes at Azrael. "I can't believe you're not on his lap yet."

"Okay, thanks." Sara wiped her hands down her apron and made her way over to him. "Hi."

"Hello." His eyes lit up to match his smile.

169

"I didn't expect to see you here."

His smile faded a little. "Is it okay?"

"Yes, very okay. I'm just busy. I can only hang out for a few minutes."

He reached out and took her hand. "I know. I just wanted to see what your life is like. I've never spent much time in the mortal world, but now that I will be, it's time I understood it more, figured out how to act." He hesitated, glancing around the shop. "I also wanted to make sure your ex-husband didn't bother you."

"I don't think he'd come by, he's probably working. Besides, I already have his money, thanks to you." Azrael wanted to protect her. The thought wrapped her in delicious warmth. She sat on the arm of his chair, ran a hand over her hair. "I'm not exactly fixed up, though."

"You look beautiful." He leaned toward her. "I want to kiss you."

She grinned. "I want to kiss you too, but I don't think that's a good idea while I'm at work."

Something passed behind his eyes, a look that reminded her of the night he'd offered to buy her a house. She knew he was thinking she didn't need this job.

She squeezed his hand. "Patience is a virtue."

"It's not one of mine." He sighed. "You're a stubborn woman."

Laughing, she tossed her head back. "See? You're learning more about me all the time." Against her better judgment, she gave him a quick kiss, dropping his hand to support herself on the arms of the overstuffed chair. "Don't pout. It ruins your bad boy look."

He slanted his eyes at her. "Bad boy?"

"You know, that whole dark and mysterious thing you have going on."

He raised a brow. "And being a bad boy is a good thing?"

"Trust me, it's very sexy."

Stretching out his long legs, he relaxed into the chair like a cat before a roaring fire. The way he looked at her made her feel naked. Or like she wanted to be naked.

"Ahem. I think I should get back to work." Otherwise, she was going to straddle his lap and kiss that wicked grin off his naughty mouth.

He started to get up, but she stopped him. "As you were. You can hang out until my shift is over. People spend hours here, it's no big deal. But you better switch to decaf or you'll be flying."

He stared at his cup.

"The caffeine, it makes you hyper. Just don't drink too much, okay?" She stood up and checked her watch. "Not long now."

When she finished her shift, she freshened up, added a little more makeup, then changed into her nicer hospital clothes. She smacked her strawberry gloss covered lips. Usually, she waited until she got there to change but she wanted to look her best for Azrael. Or at least better than she did when he'd first come in.

He stood by the side door, watching the other customers as he waited for her.

She tugged his sleeve. "I'm ready."

The moment they were outside, he turned, threaded his fingers into her hair and kissed her long and hard. His neediness made her weak. She leaned into him for support and everywhere they touched, her body flamed. She sucked in air when his mouth left hers, but held tight to his arm to steady herself. Through the glass door, Keysha gave her a thumbs up from behind the counter.

Sara doubted any gloss remained on her now tingling lips. "Wow. What was that all about?"

"You made me wait until you were no longer working." He took her hand, his eyes shining with earnest light. "I don't like to wait."

* * *

Want was not an emotion Azrael was accustomed to. However, his needs and desires had never before hinged on a mortal. Sara drove him to distraction. Just sitting across from her in the small sandwich shop, their knees touching, her eyes sparkling at him, the taste of her lips still on his, was enough to make him doubt his ability to maintain human form.

He wanted her so much parts of him ached that had never before in his existence ached.

"Are you listening to me?"

"What? Yes." He stared at his untouched food. "No. I'm sorry. My mind was elsewhere."

"Is something bothering you?" Sara sipped her drink, her rosy lips puckering around the straw. "Because you know you can tell me. Whatever it is."

"No, nothing's bothering me."

"Then what is it? You're obviously distracted."

"You." He put his sandwich down and stared at her mouth. That didn't help anything. He wiped his hands on a paper napkin. "You distract me."

Shaking his head, he picked up the sandwich she'd suggested and started eating. A Reuben, she called it. Sauce dribbled through his fingers, but he kept eating. It was good. He'd like to drip some of the sauce on her.

"I take it you mean that in a good way." Her eyes twinkled. "You distract me too."

His head came up. That was a good sign. "Don't you find this...distraction would be better off resolved?"

"Of course." She smirked. "Eventually." She dipped a French fry in a paper cup of ketchup and popped it in her mouth, smiling as she chewed.

He groaned. She was torturing him and she knew it. Not that he would push her. When she was ready, then it would be the right time. Resigned to the situation, he went back to eating. Maybe what he needed was to torture her back. But how? Being in the mortal world made him second guess every his move.

He tried ketchup on his fries, but found it too sweet so he ate them plain. Surprising how good mortal food was. Maybe Vitus could make something like this on occasion. His regular menu needed some new dishes.

A lightning flash of thought shot through his head. He stared at Sara, French fry in mid-air.

"What is it?" she asked.

He dropped the French fry back onto his plate. "Would you like to come to my house for dinner?"

Chapter Fourteen

She leaned forward. "You mean like in the Underworld?" she whispered.

"Something like that, yes." Why he hadn't thought of this sooner, he didn't know.

She sat back. "Sounds a little scary."

Maybe that was why. "There's nothing to be scared of. You'd be perfectly safe."

Her mouth bunched to one side and she made ketchup dots on the rim of her plate with a fry. "It would be interesting to see where you live. How would I..."

"I'd have to bring Pallidus for you."

The dots stopped. "Nothing could happen to me, like my soul getting trapped there or something like that?"

A woman at the next table gave Sara an odd look.

Azrael slid to the edge of his chair, bumping his knees against hers. "Nothing. Perfectly safe. You have my word."

"In that case, okay, I'd love to." She pulled a small leather bound book from her purse and paged through it. "Does it have to be dinner exactly? I'm off all day Sunday and if you picked me up after work on Saturday, I could stay over and spend the end of the weekend with you."

With a shake of her head, she closed the book. "That was dumb of me. I'm sure you have souls to—" The woman at the other table leaned closer, obviously listening. "—work to do, I mean. It's not like you get a day off."

Sara glared at the woman, who immediately retreated to her sandwich and drink.

He wanted to jump up and shout, even though the thought of doing something like that shocked him. "It's a great idea. Don't worry about my schedule, it's very adaptable."

Sara laughed. "You're smiling like a kid at Christmas." She shook her finger. "Don't get any ideas. Nothing gets unwrapped until I say it does."

"I would never assume otherwise." He tried to smooth his grin but couldn't. She was coming to his home.

And of course, Saturday night took forever to arrive. There was only so much instruction to give his staff and preparation to be done before he went to get her — especially since his home was *never* untidy or unkempt.

He did want to be sure he had everything she liked, including coffee. She seemed to have a particular fondness for the stuff, and he knew most mortals, her included, couldn't function in the morning without it.

He was early to her apartment, so he kept his Reaper form. An unknown man hanging around a woman's apartment door might arouse suspicion.

At last, her car pulled into the parking lot. Finally, she was done with work and all his. He used the shadows of the stairwell to take on his human form. She winked when she saw him, but didn't say anything as she headed toward the stairs. Once they were hidden by the stairwell he pulled her into his arms. He kissed her hello, the taste of her adding new fire to the anticipatory heat that had been building in him all day.

"Hi to you, too," she whispered when the kiss ended, her lids heavy with what he hoped was her own anticipation.

"Ready to go?"

"You bet. I just need to change and get my bag. C'mon up." He followed her into the apartment, relaxing on the couch while she changed.

She came back out dressed in jeans and an ivory top. She plopped a small overnight bag on the arm of the couch. "Okay, I'm all yours."

He'd never heard sweeter words.

His low whistle brought Pallidus through in a portal of mist. Squeezed between the sofa and dining table, the horse overwhelmed the small apartment.

She laughed. "I hope none of my neighbors can see in. Horses definitely violate the no pets over twenty pounds rule."

"Don't worry. Just like the way only you can see me, you're the only mortal who can see him." Azrael took her bag and held out his hand. "Your ride awaits."

He helped her onto Pallidus's back, then mounted behind her. "Shall we?"

Sara nodded. "I'm really looking forward to this."

"So am I." He wrapped an arm around her waist and she leaned back. He brushed the top of her head with a kiss. Tonight had to go well. He needed her in his life. Wanted her to be a part of his world in whatever way possible.

And if she'd let him, he'd give her everything she ever dreamed of.

* * *

Mist enveloped them as Pallidus took flight and Sara knew there'd be nothing to see until they came closer to their destination. And as eager as she was to see Azrael's home, she found contentment in the moment, in being back in his arms. The irony of finding a sense of safety with Death himself wasn't lost on her.

The mist swirled away sooner than expected. The land beneath them unfolded in a bruised wash of umber fields and amethyst hills. Twilight dusted the horizon with muted violet and heather.

She leaned forward to get a better look. A mansion sprawled across the land below, all curves of gray stone and rounded turrets like a Disney-inspired castle. Intricate gardens surrounded the home. Hedge mazes that seemed to have no solution wound out from the west and east ends of the building, their ordered lines tightly controlled. A wide, half-circled path in the front served as a sort of drive. In the fading light, it luminesced like a river of moonlight.

It was all very peaceful and yet a sense of melancholy lingered in the air with the perfume of old roses. His home was both beautiful and haunting.

"This is your home?" She asked not because she wasn't sure, but because she needed affirmation that he truly lived in this place.

"Yes." His voice held a note of uncertainty.

He must wonder what she thought of it. "It's beautiful," she reassured him, meaning the words down to her heart. "Like something out of a dream." And that was exactly what it was. A dreamland. No place like this could exist anywhere else but here. She couldn't wait to see it when the sun came up.

Pallidus set down on the luminous circular path. Beyond them stood the mansion's great arched double doors. Azrael slid off first, then helped her down. Gravel rolled beneath her feet. She glanced down at the odd, rounded stones that seemed to hold their own light.

"Isn't that odd?" she asked, mostly to herself. She bent and scooped up a few, rolling the soft shapes in her hand for closer inspection. Her jaw fell open. "Are these what I think they are?"

"Pearls? Yes." Azrael hefted her bag, then patted Pallidus's hindquarters. The horse trotted off toward the fields.

"You paved your driveway with pearls." She let the precious gems trickle out of her hand and back onto the ground. His driveway was wide enough for two cars and easily as long as a football field. Creating the pathway must have taken hundreds of thousands of pearls. Pearls that somehow didn't slip or roll under foot.

He shrugged. "I like the light they give off."

"You must have to replace them all the time. One big vehicle and…" She paused, realizing she had no idea what kind of automation existed in his world.

"I have no visitors."

"None?" A ghostly figure without much real shape drifted past, the barely visible face drawn and anguished.

She pointed to the thing as it disappeared around the corner of a hedge. "What was that?"

"A Shade." Before she could comment further, he swept the hand holding her bag toward the double doors while offering her his other arm. "Welcome to my home."

She rested her hand in the crook of his arm and walked with him toward the house. The Shade was a little freaky but his earlier confession still rung in her head. No visitors. What a lonely existence he must live. "So I'm the first mortal to see your home?"

"You're the first to ever step foot in my world. No mortal could be here uninvited."

The doors opened as they climbed the marble steps. He nodded toward the pale figure in the doorway. "Vitus, my butler, is a Shade, as are all the other staff, although they've been granted much more substantial forms."

He turned to her at the threshold and brought her hand to his mouth for a kiss. "My home is yours. Anything you need, you have simply to ask me or any of my staff." He squeezed her hand and smiled. "Thank you for coming."

"Thank you for inviting me." Treading where no human had ever been before gave her an odd thrill. If this was the Underworld, it wasn't all that bad. In the bright light of day it would probably be a very lovely place.

Vitus bowed and opened the doors further, revealing her first glimpse into Azrael's home.

"Oh..." she whispered. "Oh my."

The foyer beyond was awash in silver gilt moldings and decorative trim. An enormous chandelier hung from the high, frescoed ceiling like a crystal wedding cake. She stepped through the door still holding Azrael's hand. Unable to keep her gaze from roaming, she stared unabashedly, trying to take it all in. The subtle scent of spice permeated the air.

The plaster walls were the color of pale blue slate and as smooth as glass. A thick wool runner spanned the hall's length in a woodland scene of deer and pheasant. The floor itself seemed to be tiled with great squares of mother of pearl. Delicate strains of chamber music floated in from another room.

"This is gorgeous." She tore her gaze from the room long enough to meet Azrael's eyes.

He grinned, clearly pleased. "I'm glad you like it. Would you like to see the rest?"

"Yes, definitely." If the foyer looked like this, how much better could the rest of the house be?

He handed her bag to Vitus, who clutched it like a priceless object. "Take that to Sara's room, then see that dinner is underway."

The Shade nodded and disappeared.

"He doesn't talk much, does he?"

Azrael's dark gaze stayed on the spot where Vitus had been. "He doesn't talk at all. None of the Shades do. They can't." He blinked, then offered her a smile that didn't reach his eyes. "Come. I'll show you the rest."

She didn't budge. "Do all souls turn into Shades?"

"No, mostly those taken before their time."

"Like the ones Kol reaps."

"Yes." He gestured down the hall, clearly done with the topic. "Shall we?"

But she had more questions. "What happens to the other souls then?"

He dropped his hand to his side. "Some pass on to a heavenly paradise as a reward for a faithful life well lived, some pass on to Hades' Underworld—what mortals think of as Hell—to be punished for their evil ways. And some, the very youngest, are sent to the Fates to be reborn into mortal life for another chance."

"Hades? As in the god Hades?"

"Yes, but his portion of the Underworld doesn't touch this one." He raised a brow. "Any more questions?"

"No. Not for now anyway." She took his hand, her head stuffed with the information he'd just given her. "Lead on."

Each room in Azrael's house was more impressive than the last, but it reminded Sara of a museum after closing hours. The home bore little evidence of being lived in, no signs of any human touch. She chided herself for that thought. What human touch could there be in such a place? With every new and beautiful room, her heart broke a little more for Azrael. Beauty was no substitute for companionship, and clearly his mute staff couldn't supply much of that either.

They stopped at the end of a long hall filled with grandly framed mirrors and stood before two opposing sets of elaborately carved double doors. He moved to the pair on the right, rested his hand on the knob and inclined his head slightly. "Your room."

She lifted her chin and slanted her eyes to the other set of doors. "And those?"

"Mine."

He turned the knob and pushed the door open, letting her in first.

"I hope you find the space to your liking."

Her hand went to her throat. The room was a morning sunrise of blush and ivory and rose. Thick cream carpet latticed with gold covered the floor. Pale pink silk shot through with gold thread swathed the canopied bed and walls. An impressive star-shaped chandelier hung from a ceiling frescoed to resemble a dawn sky. Pinpoints of light set into the plaster picked out the constellations. Bouquets of white and shell pink roses unfurled their decadent scent into the air. If she'd designed the room herself, she wouldn't have done anything differently, not that she would have ever imagined something this beautiful.

"It's a fairytale," she breathed. Her bag, looking completely mundane and out of place, rested on the plush bed. She twisted to face him. "If you never have visitors, how is it you have a room like this?"

"It's for you." He shifted uncomfortably, not quite making eye contact.

"I understand that, but why even have such a room if no one ever comes to visit."

"It's *only* for you."

"You don't mean that this room was created for me, do you?" That couldn't be right. Would he do that? The possibility was too overwhelming. Her breath caught at being the focus of such attention.

His gaze stayed on the floor as he pointed toward a single arched door. "The guest bath is through there."

Instead of asking again, she nodded and walked through the door to see what other wonders might exist. The adjoining bath was a study in opulence. Sunk into the marble floor was a pool large enough for three or four bathers. Or one average sized mortal and one large Reaper. Steam rose in lazy swirls from the crystal blue depths, heating the room with a sensuous, inviting warmth. The urge to shed her clothes and indulge was nearly irresistible. She didn't doubt he'd follow her lead.

"It's fed from an underground hot spring."

She jumped, not so much startled by his presence as she was at being caught with her head full of wicked thoughts.

"Oh." She giggled nervously. She was alone. With him. In his house. In his world.

Every muscle in her body thrummed with the night's potential.

"I didn't mean to startle you." He leaned against the doorframe, filling the passage.

"I was just lost in how beautiful this all is." Her fingers trailed the marble ledge holding thick white towels. She ran her hand over them, not surprised by their velvety softness. Everything in his world was the best of its kind.

So what was she doing here?

He tipped his head toward the adjacent wall and the robe that hung from a hook there. "That's for you, too."

The snow-white robe bore an elaborate calligraphy S over the breast. She traced a finger over the silver embroidery. "You did do all this for me, didn't you?"

His jaw tightened, then relaxed. "And if I did?"

Was he worried he would scare her away with so much attention? Moving away from the robe, she stepped closer to splay her hand over his heart. "Then I'm a very lucky woman."

He covered her hand with his own. The contact made her want more.

"Luck has nothing to do with it." His mouth crooked. "I should probably stop cursing the Fates, though."

If he kissed her now, they'd end up in that sinful nest of a bed in the other room.

"I love you, Sara. I know you're not ready to say that back to me...maybe you'll never say it to me, but it doesn't change the way I feel."

The fullness in her heart made her head spin. Being loved like this was an intoxicating thing. She leaned in, letting him support her, and stared at their joined hands. "I think I do love you, but it scares me."

"I scare you?"

"No, not you. Loving you. I barely know what it means to be in love, let along with a man like you." She met his shining gaze and understood something new had begun between them in that moment. A course of action set into motion she was powerless to stop.

"What do you want it to mean?"

"Safety. Security. Joy. Passion. A life of happiness and contentment." She smiled. "I want it all."

He raised her fingertips and brushed them across his lips. "I can give you that and more."

She wondered about the truth of that. Not that she thought he lied, just that what he meant and what she wanted might be two different things. What about children? Were they included in his 'more'? She didn't want to delve any deeper for fear she'd ruin the time they had together. What she wanted at the moment was something far more temporal.

More physical.

More wicked.

"So..." She held his dark gaze, let her deepest desires rise into her eyes. "Your room is across the hall?"

Chapter Fifteen

The heat in Azrael's belly had nothing to do with the temperature of the guest bath. Sara's heady gaze had kindled a fire so fierce, it could burn them both down. He shoved open the doors to his chambers, waited for her to enter, then secured them again.

He tried to see the room through her eyes. His personal space was nothing like the rest of the house. No heavy tapestries or ornate gilded mirrors hung from the walls here. Clean, simple lines dictated the few pieces of furniture, his bed, the leather chaise before the fire, the writing desk and chair. Even the pattern of the rugs was simple. The colors here were born of shadow; soft grays, muted blues, some black.

She drew her hand along the leather chaise, nodding as she drifted toward the balcony. "It's very you, I have to say."

Firelight flickered in the panes of the balcony doors, outlining her where she stood peering into the dark.

Night had arrived, removing the last of twilight's soft glow.

"Is that a good thing?" He moved to stand behind her, wanting to touch her, but knowing when he did, he wouldn't stop.

"Yes," she answered without turning. "I think it is. What's beyond these doors? What's the view? I'm so turned around I don't know what direction I'm facing anymore."

He reached past, turned the knob and pushed. "The back of the house overlooks the fields and beyond to the river dividing my land from my brothers."

She walked out to the carved stone balustrades, leaning forward with her hands planted and her shoulders drawn up. "I didn't realize you all lived in the same place, but I guess that makes sense, doesn't it?"

After a few steps, he stopped with enough distance between them to assure they made it to dinner. "There is only one Underworld, but my brothers' lands are very different from mine."

"I like your home." She tipped her head back to the star encrusted sky. At least his world had that much to offer her. "They look close enough to touch," she murmured. "So much bigger and brighter than at home."

"You outshine them."

She laughed softly. "You say the sweetest things."

He stayed were he was, although he longed to pin her against the balustrades and discover the wonders of mortal flesh. He swallowed hard. "We should go down for dinner."

She turned, replanted her hands on the rail and stared into him as though she knew he struggled to keep from ravishing her and didn't care. Maybe she didn't.

Maybe she struggled too.

"Hmm, yes, dinner." She glanced down at her clothes. "I don't think I'm dressed appropriately for dinner in a house like this."

"You look fine." Better than fine, and speaking of dinner, good enough to eat. He wanted his hands on her skin, his mouth on her—

Her head snapped up. "Did you just growl?"

"Must have been my stomach." He motioned back toward the doors. "Shall we?" The sooner they ate, the sooner they could have dessert.

As he'd requested, his staff had set a small round table in the great room. The dining room was too large, the table too big. Being close to Sara was paramount.

From the crystal stemware to the solid sterling settings, the table was perfect. Shades might not make great company, but they were excellent house staff. He pulled out her chair to seat her, then seated himself.

Vitus came from the shadows to fill their wine glasses, then the meal service began. Sara gushed over the wine, the food, the place settings...it seemed he had done everything right.

Until dessert.

Her smile faded slightly as Vitus set the pear poached in champagne and drizzled with raspberry sauce before her.

"Something wrong?" Azrael asked.

"No, everything's wonderful." She nudged the pear with her spoon.

"You don't like fruit?"

"I love fruit. It's very good for you."

He grinned, suddenly aware of his error. "But it's not chocolate, is it?"

She smiled sheepishly. "Chocolate is a weakness. But ignore me. This is lovely, really."

He sat back, biting the inside of his cheek to keep from laughing. "What would your ideal dessert be? More of that coffee ice cream?"

"You can never go wrong with coffee chocolate chip, but for a meal like this it's probably a little too ordinary. Maybe something like one of those gooey chocolate volcano cakes, or some sort of triple chocolate mousse."

He nodded toward her plate. "You mean like that?"

Glancing down at the mound of chocolate decadence now in front of her, she exhaled sharply. "How did you do that?"

"This is my world." He shrugged, watching with pleasure as she dug in. "My power here is almost limitless."

"Mmmmm..." She pulled the empty fork from between her lips and sighed. "That's the most amazing thing I've ever tasted." She took another bite, licking an errant dribble of chocolate sauce from her bottom lip.

Azrael's groin tightened as if she'd licked him.

"If this is life in the Underworld, I think I'm ready to die."

He straightened. "Don't say that, Sara. Mortal life must run its course or—"

"I know, I know." She waved her fork at him. "The whole Shade thing. I was just kidding. But I do like it here. At first I thought it was a little gloomy, but now I'm thinking it's just..." She waved her fork again. "Atmospheric."

Maybe she knew there was no daylight here? He let that thought be, if only to keep from telling her the truth of his sunless world.

She scooped up another bite of dessert and offered it to him. "You really should try this. It's delicious."

He leaned forward. "You're the only sweet I want."

193

She fluttered her lids and fanned herself with her hand. "My, my, Mr. Reaper, you do know how to woo a girl, don't you?" She laughed, the most wonderful sound ever to echo in the halls of his home. "I probably shouldn't tell you this, but I'm pretty much a sure thing."

"A sure thing?" Some mortal expressions eluded him.

She finished another bite of dessert, then shook her head, her cheeks coloring. "Never mind."

She tipped her head toward the piano. "Is that just for show or do you play?"

"I play."

"Really?" Her brows lifted in shock.

"And that surprises you because?"

"I don't know...it just never occurred to me that the Grim Reaper would play the piano. And human guys who look like you are usually into sports and working out and, well, not playing the piano." She stared at him expectantly. "Aren't you going to play something for me?"

"What? No." He'd never played for anyone. Certainly, the Shades overheard when he played, but they didn't count. His music was private. Just for him. And probably not very good.

"No? Why not?" A bemused smirk bent her mouth.

"It's not something I do for...guests."

"Well, of course it isn't. You've never had guests. Now you do." She stood up, walked to piano and drew her finger across the keys in a slow scale. "And I want to hear you play something."

He sighed and crossed his arms, forcing back a grin. "Maybe this is *why* I don't have guests."

Narrowing her eyes did nothing to diminish the mischievous light in them. "Yes, I think you're right. Your lack of hospitality must have something to do with it." She plopped down on the bench and plunked out a halted rendition of *Chopsticks*.

"As you wish," he called over the racket as he stood.

She stopped playing and scooted to one end of the bench, patting the empty spot. "It's all yours, maestro."

"Chocolate makes you wicked."

"You should see what champagne does to me."

He focused his attention and instantly an ice bucket on a stand appeared beside the piano, complete with a frosted bottle of bubbly. Two glasses rested on the piano top.

"Very impressive." She plunked a key. "Play now, drink later." She leaned in to whisper in his ear. "If you're really good, maybe we'll drink that bottle in the tub." She laughed and blushed, covering her mouth with her hand.

He focused a second time, mentally adding a plate of fine chocolates to every room in the house, including both of their nightstands. When the night was over, she'd be too tired to blush. He flexed his fingers. Channeling everything he felt for Sara, he began to play.

The music poured out of him, lush and aching. Full of longing and desire. It suffused the room. The house. His world.

His woman.

Sara's eyes were closed, her head tipped back and to the side. The flush had slipped from her cheeks and down to the glimpse of skin visible above the neckline of her ivory top. Dessert indeed.

Her hand lifted to her throat, her fingers touching the pendant he'd given her.

He played on, weaving his power into the notes until he could feel them sweep across her skin as if his hands glided over her. He became the music and she became his instrument. Softer and slower, then more insistent, he played her until she quivered beside him.

The heat of her frenzied body radiated into him as he finished. Not until the last notes died away did she open her eyes.

"What...what was that?"

Foreplay, he thought. "Didn't you like it?"

"Like it? I think I almost..." She trailed off, fanning herself. "Never mind." She exhaled hard. "I've never heard music that sounded like that. I could feel it in every cell of my body."

He commanded new music to fill the air, something slow and deliberate. At the first notes, he stood and held out his hand to her.

"Dance with me." It was a command, not a request.

"I'm not sure I can stand just yet. I feel strangely weak." She smoothed a hand down her thigh. "Too much wine or something."

"I'll support you."

She took his hand, let him pull her up. Her gaze went sideways, to the enormous gilt mirror on the side wall. "I'm not dressed for dancing."

Cradling her chin in his fingers, he turned her face to his. "And how should you be dressed?"

"In a beautiful gown, with jewels, and my hair done up. Something more romantic than jeans."

"Something like this?" He curved her back toward the mirror so she could see what he'd done.

"Oh, it's beautiful." Her voice was little more than a breathy whisper as she surveyed the elegant red gown she now wore. Her fingers trailed the circlet of diamonds and rubies at her neck, drops of the same at her ears. She turned her head to better see her upswept hair. "I feel like Pretty Woman."

"Who?" He worked a little magic on his own attire just as she came around in his direction.

"You know, the movie with-" She stopped when she saw him, her eyes alight with undeniable desire. "You should always wear a tux."

"Always?"

"At least for a little while." Her hand grazed his lapel, pausing on his chest. "I feel like a princess."

"You could be queen." He pulled her into his arms, his hands possessively at her waist.

"Queen?"

"Of this world. Marry me, Sara." He wasn't sure where the words had come from, but he'd never meant anything more in his life. "I never knew what life could be until I met you, and now I know an existence without you isn't something I want to face."

"Is it even possible?" A thin line of moisture rimmed her hopeful eyes.

"I can take human form as often as you need me to."

"I'm not sure...there are so many questions I need to ask..."

"Like what? Ask me."

"You don't understand, there are things I need—"

"Surely tonight should help you see what I am capable of. There's nothing I can't give you, Sara."

She swallowed. The tears were closer to spilling. "Even children?"

Chapter Sixteen

All emotion vanished from Azrael's face except one. Panic. Just as Sara had expected, he hadn't counted on her wanting children. They hadn't fit into Ray's timeline either.

"Forget I said anything." She spun away, not wanting him to see the hurt she knew must be shining in her eyes.

But he held her tight. "No, Sara, it's not what you think."

She shook her head, inhaled to calm herself.

"You caught me off guard," he said. She glanced up as he continued. "You must understand that for a Reaper, children never even seem like a possibility worth thinking about. But in my human form..." He hesitated. The beginnings of a smile crept along his mouth. "I don't see why it wouldn't be possible. And wonderful." He laughed. "Might be a bit of an odd life for them, living between both worlds, but you'd be a great mother."

He tugged her close again. "Say yes, Sara. Say yes."

"I don't think odd begins to cover it." She scrunched her mouth to one side, a spring of emotion welling in her. "But odd has never stopped me before."

His jaw unhinged. "Does that mean..."

"Yes." She nodded, unable to keep the joy from her face. "I'll marry you."

He swept her into his arms, twirling her around and making her laugh. He stopped suddenly, his brow furrowed. "I didn't think this through very well."

Her heart sank in preparation of his next words and a shuddered sigh escaped her lips. What now?

"I didn't get a ring."

He winked, lifted her hand and kissed the joint of her ring finger, leaving behind a sparkling diamond fit for a princess. Smaller diamonds accented the round center stone. This was really happening. She was engaged.

"Do you like it?" he asked.

"Like it? I love it." She took a closer look and her heart made a quick ascent back to her throat. "Oh, Azrael. That's...that's...huge! I can't possibly accept something that extravagant."

"Why not?" His expression grew stern. "As my wife, you must know I will not abide you having anything less than the best. It's a husband's job to spoil his wife."

She almost laughed, wishing Ray could hear those words. She tilted her hand, sending a shower of sparks into the air. "No one will even think it's real. At least not on me." She held the ring closer. "It's breathtaking." She shoved her hand out again. "Like something you'd see on a movie star." Giddiness threatened to overwhelm her. "Or on the finger of woman whose husband likes to spoil her senseless."

He laughed. "I'd be happy to make the stone smaller."

She clutched her hands together, covering the ring. "I'll learn to deal."

"I don't doubt it." He twirled her away, then in against him, her back to his chest. A happy sigh escaped her and she tipped her head to look up at him, leaning against his hard body. "I can't believe this is happening."

"Believe it, because it is." He kissed the side of her neck until she squealed. "In fact, let's make it real. Right now. Tonight."

She twisted around to look at him. "You mean get married right now?"

"Yes. There are places in your world where mortals marry impulsively all the time."

Her brows knit together. "You mean...Vegas?"

"Yes. We'll go there." He took her hand as if to lead her somewhere, then hesitated. "Unless you'd prefer something more elaborate? More traditional?"

Planning her first wedding had nearly put her in the nut house. So many details to contend with, so many preparations for a single day that sped by like a bullet train. Not to mention the expense. And for what? A few hard years that culminated in divorce anyway? She shook her head. "I've done that. Didn't really work the way I thought it would. I think this time it should be different." She squeezed his hand. "Let's go tear that town up."

* * *

"Oh...wow..." Sara inhaled as the bellman opened the doors to the Wynn's Salon Suite. She and Azrael had only brought a small bag apiece, but apparently a couple grand a night got you a bellman regardless of the amount of luggage you carried. Maybe they shouldn't have changed into street clothes before they'd come. A ball gown and tux seemed more suited to the exquisite suite.

"The salon suite is one of Wynn's finest. I trust you will find it very comfortable. Of course, if you need anything while you're here, simply call your personal concierge and he'll gladly see to it, twenty-four hours a day." The bellman handed a card to Azrael, then swept off to the bedroom with their bags.

"This place is bigger than my apartment." She stood before the wall to ceiling windows overlooking the Strip.

"That will change when we get back."

She glanced over her shoulder. The look on his face brooked no argument. But then, they were going to be married. Why shouldn't they buy a new home together? "A place that overlooks the river would be nice."

He smiled. "Whatever you want."

A knock thumped the door. The bellman came out of the bedroom and answered it before either of them moved. "Ah, Philippe, there you are."

The bellman turned to face them. "This is Philippe, your personal concierge. I'll be going now, unless there is anything else I can do for you." He stood expectantly by the door.

"We're fine. Goodbye," Azrael said.

The bellman didn't move.

Trying not to smirk, Sara went to Azrael's side and whispered in his ear. "He wants a tip."

Azrael peeled a hundred off the roll in his pocket and gave it to the man. "Thank you."

The bellman smiled but didn't freak out like Sara expected him to. Welcome to Vegas.

"Have a wonderful night." He tipped his hat on his way out the door.

Philippe bowed his head slightly. "Is there anything I can get you for this evening? Dinner reservations? Show tickets, perhaps?"

Azrael looked at her. She shrugged. "Why not? We're here, let's have fun."

"Both then," he told the concierge. "A very romantic restaurant and the very best show. We're here to get married. I want this to be special."

Philippe broke out in a wide grin. "Married? That's one of my specialties. Have you already made your arrangements or would you like some assistance?"

Sara felt her face heat. "Actually, this was very spur of the moment. We haven't arranged anything. I don't even have a dress."

Philippe came to her side and taking her hand in his, patted it gently. "Not to worry my dear. I am at your service." Releasing her hand, he gave Azrael his attention. "If I may ask, what is your budget? I can tailor plans to suit any dollar amount."

"Money doesn't matter. Just make her happy."

"Very good, sir."

From the inside pocket of his jacket, Philippe produced a small leather-bound notebook and pen. He opened it to a blank page and handed it to her. "If you would be so kind as to jot your sizes down for me, I'll have some things brought up for you to try on."

She took it and started writing. He clasped his hands behind his back while he waited. "What day would you like the ceremony to take place, sir?"

"Tomorrow."

"Very good. How many guests will be attending?"

"None," Azrael said.

"An intimate ceremony is very romantic. I would be happy to serve as your witness, should you desire."

"That would be fine."

"I believe we'll be able to provide you with a very special day. The Wynn prides itself on exceptional service."

Sara held the notebook out to him. "I think those are right. I haven't been dress shopping in a long time."

"Not to worry. We have a seamstress available for alterations." He held the pen ready to write. "And for you, sir, a tuxedo or a suit?"

"Neither. I don't need—" Sara frowned at him. "A tuxedo would do nicely."

Philippe scribbled something. "Your size, sir?"

"I have no idea."

"Hmm. I'd say a 42 long, athletic cut, but I'll send a few sizes on either side of that." He made more notes. "Anything else I should know? Details of any kind?"

Sara grinned and gave in to her impulses. "I like roses. And chocolate cake with coffee ice cream. And maybe a harpist. Or flutes. I like violins, too. And champagne."

More scribbling, punctuated by the sharp tap of lead on paper. "Wonderful, wonderful." He tucked the notebook away. "I'll take care of everything." He checked his watch. "I'll have your dinner reservations taken care of in twenty minutes. Your show tickets will be at the will call window. Is there anything else I can do for you?"

"Yes." Azrael's eyes twinkled with an unusual light. "I'd like a word with you outside."

Philippe nodded to Sara. "I will see you tomorrow. Have a good evening."

"Thank you, you too." What on earth could Azrael be up to? She watched the two men walk out together, then Azrael shut the door. She thought about trying to listen through the door, but let them be. No use in spoiling a potential surprise.

She explored the rest of the suite, making a mental note to take advantage of the big soaking tub in the marble drenched bathroom. She plopped down onto the cloud-like bed, sinking into the thick covers. Sweeping her arms over the satiny comforter, she tried to take in the reality of her new life.

Tonight there would be more than sleeping taking place in this bed. A delicious shiver sent heat down her spine.

The sound of the door shutting barely registered in the bedroom. She sat up as Azrael walked in. She wondered if the thoughts in her head showed on her face.

"I told Philippe we needed clothes for dinner. He said there are stores right in the hotel. He'll leave our tickets and reservation info at the front desk. We can pick it up when we're ready." He held out his hand to her. "Let's go get something appropriate for our night out."

She took his hand, let him pull her up. "Are you trying to spoil me?"

"Trying to? I thought I was."

"You are."

"Good, because I don't plan on stopping." He kissed her softly, his lips brushing hers.

"I could get used to this." She laughed as he handed her purse to her and tugged her toward the door. "If all mortal men were as eager to shop as you are, there'd probably be a lot less divorce in the country."

He shut the door behind them, then pushed the elevator call button. "It's not the shopping, trust me. It's watching you have fun."

"Really?" She tapped a finger against her chin. "So it wouldn't matter to you if I was trying on lingerie or trench coats?"

The elevator doors slid open behind her. He lowered his brows, dipping his chin to make eye contact. "I wouldn't go that far."

Half an hour later she was wearing a jaw-dropping little black dress from Chanel and a killer pair of Manolo Blahnik stilettos that together cost more than her first car. She did one final twirl in the mirror while Azrael paid the clerk. Had her legs always looked so good? The idea of feeling like a million bucks had never been more understandable. If this was how the other half lived, she was all for it.

She hooked her arm through his and they strolled through the Esplanade. Azrael seemed fascinated by the myriad of colors and patterns on the floor and ceiling. She was so intent on watching him, she didn't realize they'd entered another shop until the flooring changed underfoot.

Security guards flanked the entrance of the jewelry store. An older man behind one of the glass cases greeted them with a smile. "Good evening. Welcome to Petrelli's."

"Hi." She glanced back at Azrael. He'd already given her an over the top ring, so he must want something for himself. She almost smacked her forehead. Of course! She'd completely forgotten he needed a wedding band.

He scooped his arm behind her and around her waist, nodding to the man. "Good evening. Philippe told me you sell only the best quality diamonds."

The man smiled, obviously pleased. "Yes, sir, that's true. Only the most exquisite pieces make it into our cases. Is there something particular I can show you?"

Azrael's hand went to the small of her back. "Anything she wants."

"I don't need anything. You've spent enough already." Sara shook her head. "The only thing we need is a wedding band for you."

"Good idea, but..." He traced the shell of her ear with his finger. "You need earrings." He lifted her hand and kissed her wrist. "And a bracelet. Pick out whatever you want, then we'll look at wedding bands." He gave her a sly grin. "We're not leaving until you do, so if you want to be responsible for us missing our reservation..." He shrugged.

"You're rotten, you know that? Two can play this game." She laughed, turning her attention to the man waiting on them. "Show me your most expensive diamond earrings and bracelet, then I'll look at your men's wedding bands."

The spark in the man's eyes was unmistakable. He moved to a case on the far wall and unlocked the cabinet. He slid out a creamy velvet tray, then presented it to them. "These diamond cluster earrings are fifteen carats of pear, marquis and round cuts, E color, VVS clarity. The bracelet..." He reached into the case, retrieving a blinding circle of fire and adding it to the tray. "Is another twenty-nine carats, same quality diamonds. All set in platinum. The finest pieces in the shop at the moment."

She reached for the bracelet, but he beat her to it, sliding the bracelet onto her wrist and fastening it.

"It is only outshined by your beauty, miss."

"I don't know about tha—"

"We'll take it. And the earrings," Azrael said.

She gave him a *hold on* look. "You don't even know how much they are."

Azrael turned his head toward the clerk expectantly.

"I would be happy to offer you both pieces for $200."

"$200? I thought these were diamonds?" Not that it mattered, cubic zirconia was fine with her.

"Thousand, miss. Two hundred thousand."

Her knees buckled. "What?" The word hissed out of her like air leaking from a balloon. "We haven't even picked out a wedding band yet."

Smiling, the man pulled out a small tray. "I have a nice selection of men's wedding bands. I'd be happy to include one in the price I quoted."

Azrael dropped a stack of bills on the counter. "Have the boxes sent to the Salon suite. She'll wear the pieces out."

Chapter Seventeen

The pleasures of the mortal life had become crystal clear in the course of the evening out with Sara. The food and drink surpassed Azrael's expectations. The show left him wondering if some mortals had not indeed been born with powers beyond their natural abilities.

And being at Sara's side, as her husband-to-be, had allowed the pure, shining joy of a life with her to fill his world with a light unlike anything he'd ever known. His need for her had become his blood. It thrummed through his veins, hot and heavy. She infused him so completely that every moment in time that had come before her was forgotten. She was his here and now. His reason for tomorrow.

Her fragrant warmth curled around him as she pressed against him in the elevator.

"I had the most wonderful time of my life tonight," she murmured. "But tomorrow will be even better, because tomorrow we'll be married." She laughed, soft and drowsy. "I can't believe it, but it's true and I'm happier than I thought possible. I love you, Az."

He smiled at her shortening of his name. It was intimate and personal and affectionate, the exact opposite of what Kol implied when he used it. "I love you, too. And I feel the same about this night. And tomorrow. Especially tomorrow." He lifted her chin and brought his lips to hers. She tasted of wine and chocolate and desire.

She sank into him further, parting her mouth to take his kiss with a hushed moan.

The elevator chimed. The doors whooshed open. Without breaking the kiss, he scooped her into his arms and strode the few steps across the hall to their room. He opened the door with the keycard, wishing his powers weren't so limited in mortal form, then pushed through and nudged it shut again with his foot.

"I need you, Sara." The huskiness of his voice surprised him.

She nodded, her lips flush with their kiss. "I know. I need you, too."

He carried her into the bedroom and set his precious cargo gently on the bed. Just as he moved away, she threaded her fingers into his hair, pulling him back down.

She crushed her mouth against his with a hunger that stirred his body beyond control. He had thought to take this slowly, with great gentleness and tempered passion, to show her how careful he would always be with her. "Sara, I—"

"No, Az, I can't wait." Her words came out heated and breathy. "I want you right now. Do you understand? Right now."

She tipped her head back into the coverlet, moaning, shuttering her eyes. "I'll beg if I have to."

"That won't be necessary." He loosed the fierce need that had been building in him from the first moment they'd crossed paths and bent his head to the pale, exposed column of her neck. His tongue trailed her flesh, causing her to shiver and moan again.

Her hands fisted in his shirt. She arched up, pressing her breasts against him. His teeth scuffed her collarbone. With one hand, he found the strap of her dress and tugged it down.

She pushed him away. "Take your shirt off. I want to look at you." She laughed lightly, throwing her head back as though she amused herself. "Apparently, lust makes me bossy."

He rose to his knees and unbuttoned his shirt, aroused by her commands and the newfound boldness that had taken hold of her. "Yes, mistress."

She blushed hard, but her gaze never left him. "You're beautiful, you know that? Like a Greek god carved in marble." She exhaled. "I can't believe you're mine."

Tossing his shirt aside, he bent back over her, a palm at either side of her head. "I'm glad you approve. Now I'm going to devour you like I've wanted to since we met."

"Oh no, you don't." She shook her head and pushed at him again. "You're not done."

He cocked a brow. "Of course I'm not done. I haven't even started."

"I mean those." She pointed down between them. "Lose the pants, nice and slow. I want to enjoy this."

Slanting his mouth across hers, he kissed her hard, then rose back up to his knees and began unbuckling his belt. His sweet Sara had a decidedly wicked seam. He could barely believe how good the Fates had been to him.

"I think you shall have champagne with every meal from now on."

* * *

A slipstream of sun woke Sara. She yawned and rolled over, arms outstretched in search of the man who'd kept her up all night. The bed beside her was empty.

She opened her eyes and pushed up onto her elbows. "Azrael?"

Not a half second later, he appeared in the doorway, a steaming cup of coffee in his hand. "I thought I'd be back before you woke up."

She ran a hand through her hair, knowing what a mess it must be but hardly caring. "Hi, handsome." She tipped her chin at the cup he carried toward her. "Is that for me?"

"Yes." He sat on the edge of the bed and handed the coffee over. As she sipped, one of his hands tunneled beneath the covers to stroke his fingers down her thigh. Instantly, her body hummed to life for a reason that had nothing to do with caffeine. Last night might have been his first time, but he'd done everything right. Oh, *so* right.

She swallowed another sip of the delicious liquid, the heat from the coffee no match for the heat building elsewhere. "Do you have an off switch?"

Grinning, he shook his head. "Not around you." He slid his hand out from beneath the covers. "I guess the champagne's worn off."

She groaned softly, pressed the heel of her palm to one temple. "Trust me, it's not entirely gone. I think I have a little bit of a hangover." She prayed that was all the dull throb in her head was and not one of her usual day-killing migraines. Today was her wedding day. She had no time for a headache.

"Should I get you something else?" Concern darkened his eyes.

She lifted her coffee cup. "I'll be fine after I finish this." She downed another sip. "And take a long, hot shower." She fluttered her lashes. "Care to join me?" There were other ways to get rid of a headache; she'd just never had that particular remedy quite so available before.

To the Wynn's credit, the water stayed hot through four orgasms. Azrael showed no signs of cooling, either.

A ringing phone got them out of the shower and into towels. Wisps of steam tailed him into the bedroom when he went to answer it. She wrapped her hair up in another towel and followed him with her gaze, unable to take her eyes off a single water droplet making its way down the ladder of his stomach.

"Hello? Yes, thank you." He covered the mouthpiece. "It's Philippe. He wants to send us breakfast before the clothes come to be fitted. What would you like?"

"Mmm...two eggs over easy, bacon, hash browns and pancakes with some kind of fruit on top. And whipped cream. And orange juice."

When his eyes rounded in surprise, she shrugged a still damp shoulder and replied, "What? I worked up an appetite."

"That makes two of us." He doubled the order when he relayed it to Philippe, then hung up and walked back into the bathroom, standing behind her in front of the mirror. His mouth found the curve of her shoulder while his hands griped her hips, drawing her backside against his groin.

She paused, moisturizer-laden hands mid-air, to stare at him in the glass. "Again?"

"Mmm-hmm." His words vibrated through her skin and into her core. He lifted his head to stare back at her, a devilish gleam lighting his eyes. "Breakfast won't be here for half an hour and I'm hungry now." The gleam dimmed. "Unless you're not feeling well enough?"

A deliciously wicked tingle swept through her. Being desired was a wonderful thing. The stuff of any woman's dreams. He'd drenched her in diamonds and designer clothes, wined her, dined her, and given her unbelievable amounts of pleasure. How could she say no to anything he wanted? She winked at him. "I feel plenty well enough." Not exactly the truth, but he was worth it.

Twenty minutes later, panting and limp, she sprawled on the bed in a fog of bliss. He brought her a robe, helped her into it, then went to get her another cup of coffee.

"Maybe we should skip the fancy clothes and get married like this," she said as she took the cup from him.

"In bathrobes?" He slanted his eyes away as though he were thinking about it. "I like it. Much less to get you out of once the ceremony is over."

She laughed. "Sex has corrupted your brain."

"Too late. You already said yes." He squeezed her knee. "Breakfast will be here soon. I have some work I need to do, but I'll only be gone the equivalent of five of your minutes."

"Okay, I guess I should put some clothes on then." She got up to get dressed, setting her coffee cup on the nightstand.

He handed her a small roll of bills. "Take this."

"What for?"

"Just in case." He kissed her, then flashed to his Reaper form and disappeared.

And although she knew he'd only be gone a short time, a small sorrow welled up. She almost shut it away, but instead she let the bittersweet rush fill her as proof that she loved him. By the end of the day, he would be hers completely and nothing could ever separate them after that.

This might be the one marriage where "until death do us part" wouldn't apply.

Happiness renewed, she dressed and put on a little makeup, letting her hair air dry. A knock at the door brought her out of the bathroom. Azrael was already there opening it, letting room service in.

She sidled up to him, hugging his arm. "Is it silly that I missed you?"

He kissed the top of her head. "I like being missed."

They ate breakfast quickly, finishing just as the selection of wedding dresses and suits arrived. Philippe followed the racks in.

"Good morning. How are the bride and groom today? Nervous? Excited?" His entire face lit up. He either loved weddings or planning them.

"Very well. Not nervous, are we?" Azrael looked at her, waiting for an affirmation.

"No, not nervous at all. Excited. Ready to get married." And she was, more than she'd ever been. Life had never been so perfect.

"Wonderful!" Philippe gestured to the young woman with the rack of dresses. "This is Ryka. She's going to help you with the dresses. Anything that needs alterations, she can handle. Why don't you two use the bedroom and we'll fit the suit out here? Bad luck for the groom to see the bride and all that."

"Sounds good." Sara shook her finger at Azrael. "No peeking."

Once Ryka had the rack of dresses in, Sara shut the bedroom door. "Hi, I'm Sara. Nice to meet you."

"You too." Beneath artfully sculpted brows, the brunette beauty's eyes lifted at the corners, cat-like and exotic. "Your fiancé is hot stuff, if you don't mind me saying so."

Sara laughed. "I don't mind. I happen to think so too."

Ryka gripped the rack's supporting bar. "Why don't you look through these, pick out the ones you like best and try them on? If there's nothing here that suits you, I can get another rack in about an hour."

"I'm sure there will be something perfect. There must be a hundred dresses here." Sara drifted her hand across the garment bag wrapped gowns.

"Forty-two actually. Plus a good selection of veils. Also, I didn't know if you'd have the right foundation garments, so I brought some of those too." She held up a small bag. "The dresses are hung in order of the simplest to the most elaborate." Ryka pulled the first one out and unzipped the bag. "This is a crystal white shantung silk, strapless corset-style top with lacing down the back. No adornments, no beading, nothing. It's a great dress if you've got some really stunning jewelry to wear with it or you can pair it with a really over the top veil."

Sara went to the dresser and took the black velvet boxes from the top drawer. "I have these." She opened them to show Ryka the diamond earrings and bracelet.

"Holy Mother of God." Ryka glanced at her then back at the jewels. "Sorry. You'd think working in Vegas I'd get used to seeing rocks like that, but up close they're always so much more impressive. Nice. Very nice. And great with a dress like this." She shooed Sara toward the bathroom. "Go try it on."

Five minutes later and Sara was done struggling with the lacing down the back. She came out holding the dress up with her arms pinned to her sides. "How are you supposed to put a dress like this on without help?"

"You're not. Here, let me."

Once laced in, Sara turned before the mirror. The dress hugged her body in a way that was both elegant and sexy. She added the earrings and bracelet.

Ryka nodded. "That's exactly what I was talking about. You just need one thing." She rummaged through the garment bags, finally lifting free a long wisp of crystal-studded tulle. With a few deft movements, she anchored it into Sara's hair and fluffed the veil out to fall gracefully around her face.

"There." Ryka stood back, obviously pleased.

"Wow," Sara whispered. She couldn't believe the woman in white staring back from the mirror was her. "I don't think I need to try anything else on."

"I agree." Ryka looped her arm over the rack's hanging bar. "You look amazing. You're going to knock him dead when he sees you."

Sara smiled. "I don't think there's much chance of that."

Chapter Eighteen

As the first strands of Pachelbel's Canon in D lifted from the string quartet, Azrael turned to watch Sara glide down the rose petal strewn aisle of the outdoor chapel.

His breath caught in his throat at first sight of her. Everything else fell away in that moment and his world narrowed down to her, his angel in white. What else was there but the woman who held his heart and gave his life reason?

Step by step, she narrowed the space between them, shortening the time before they would be bound together. A sharp, beautiful pain filled him. He had no name for it, but felt as though he could laugh and cry at the same time.

Standing beside him now, she gazed up from beneath the veil, eyes large and liquid, and mouthed the words, "I love you."

He smiled. Nearly laughed, his joy was so great. "And I you," he whispered back.

The officiate spoke his words, they responded with their vows, and the pronouncement was made. In a fleeting instant, they were man and wife. Death and his mortal lover. He lifted her veil and kissed her sweet mouth tenderly.

Philippe, who had stood as their witness, smiled as they broke the kiss. "You two make a lovely couple. I wish you the happiest of lives togeth—"

Slow, deliberate clapping interrupted Philippe's congratulations.

Azrael looked toward the sound. Kol leaned against one of the ivy-wrapped columns, his hands meeting in a determined beat. Chronos stood beside him, both in their mortal forms. Not that Kol looked any different.

Kol stopped clapping and wiped at a tear that wasn't there. "Touching. Is there an open bar?"

"I didn't know you invited them," Sara whispered.

"I didn't," he answered. He glanced back at the officiate who eyed Kol with a healthy nervousness. Philippe stared as well. Azrael cleared his throat to get their attention off Kol. "Thank you for performing the ceremony. If you don't mind, we'd like to be alone now."

The officiate nodded and took off. Philippe did not. "I can call security if you wish."

"No, thank you. We're fine. We just need some privacy."

224

Philippe nodded, looking unconvinced. "As you wish." He kept his gaze on Kol as he left.

Kol, who'd obviously been watching from behind his ever-present dark glasses, laughed and headed for the cake table.

Chronos shook his head and walked toward them. "What do you think this marriage is going to accomplish?"

"What do you care?" Azrael bit back, wrapping a protective arm around Sara. "My life. My way. And if I'm happy, so be it."

"Sucker." Kol dragged his finger through the buttercream icing, leaving a stripe of chocolate cake visible, and stuck it into his mouth.

Chronos sighed. "Until she dies and one of us has to reap her soul. And if it's not you—"

"Stop talking about Sara like she'd not here. And it will be me that reaps her soul." Somehow, he would make sure her soul came through him. Then he had a chance of holding on to it, of keeping her with him.

"You don't know that." Chronos dipped his head at Sara. "I'm sorry to interrupt, I know what importance a wedding day holds for mortal women, but my brother has done a very foolish thing."

She straightened a bit. "Love often *is* a very foolish thing. That doesn't mean it's not worth it."

A slight, sad smile bent Chronos' mouth. "On one hand it is a very noble thing that you love my brother knowing him for who he is, however, on the other hand, it is unspeakably cruel."

"Cruel? That I love him? How?" Indignation flashed in her eyes, more brilliant than the diamonds adorning her.

Chronos stepped closer. "You will live for perhaps eighty or ninety years, if the Fates are kind. You will grow gray and bent, weakening as the days press you back down into the earth you were born from."

His eyes slanted at Azrael, then back to her. "Azrael, still unchanged, will have to watch you succumb to the ravages of time, unable to stop the inevitable. And then, when you die, he will be left with nothing but memories and an eternity alone in which to grieve you."

His mouth thinned into a hard line. "That is what I mean by cruel."

She looked stricken, although Azrael sensed she fought to hide her reaction. Liquid rimmed her eyes. Biting her lip, she glanced at Azrael. "I'm so sorry. I didn't understand—"

"Hush now." He took her face in his hands. He had to make her see that the truth his brother spoke didn't matter. "My beautiful Sara. What my brother fails to understand is that whatever time we have together is worth what follows after. I love you. And I will not trade what we have for anything." He brushed a kiss across her lips before releasing her and turning his attention back to Chronos. "If you cannot be happy for me, you need to leave. Today is a day of celebration."

"You've made your peace with the future then?" Chronos narrowed his eyes as if he wouldn't believe Azrael's answer no matter what it was.

"Yes. And I chose to live in the present." Azrael didn't need his brothers' approval, but that didn't stop him from wanting it. "You can celebrate this day with us, or leave."

"I'm staying." Kol waved the bottle of champagne he'd been drinking out of. In his other hand, he held a chunk of wedding cake. "Vegas is my kind of town."

"Then I will stay too." Chronos shrugged. "You may need a hand with him." He turned away, then hesitated and faced Sara. "I'm sorry for upsetting you, it wasn't my intention. I will try to be more mindful of mortal emotions when you are present. You are a lovely woman and you've done something no other mortal has been capable of." He smiled. "You've gotten my brother to have some fun."

Extending his hand, he offered her a small, hinged box of red leather. "Please accept this as a token of my apology. A wedding gift will follow."

She accepted the box and opened it. Black pearl and diamond drops gleamed in the Nevada sun. "You reapers sure know your way around a jewelry store. They're beautiful. Thank you."

"They'll look lovely on you." Azrael nodded, pleased with his brother's gift and Sara's willingness to forgive.

"You're welcome." Chronos called over his shoulder for Kol. "Come here."

Kol sauntered over without releasing the bottle of champagne. He took a long swig, then wiped the back of his hand across his mouth. "What now?"

"Your gift," Chronos urged.

"Huh? Oh yeah." Kol shook the icing off his fingers and dug inside his long black coat. "Here." He handed Sara another red leather box, this one a flat square, larger than Chronos' offering.

She opened it and gasped again. A strand of matching black pearls rested on ivory velvet. "They're absolutely stunning. Thank you so much." She looked at Kol with an odd smile on her face. "There's not a curse on these or anything, is there?"

"No." Kol had the audacity to look hurt when Chronos and Azrael laughed. "Whatever." He jerked his thumb back toward the empty courtyard. "Where are all the drunk bridesmaids?"

Azrael rolled his eyes. "There is no wedding party. It was to be Sara and myself alone."

Kol shrugged. "Suit yourself. I'm out of here. This party blows compared to what's happening on the Strip." Shards of black smoke glimmered where he'd stood, then dissipated into nothingness.

"Perhaps I should take my leave as well since it was not your intention to entertain guests." Chronos clapped Azrael on the shoulder.

"You don't have to go," Sara countered.

"Thank you, but you should be able to enjoy this day together. I would only be in your way." Before she could say another word, Chronos dissolved into a million tiny pieces and blew away on the wind like a handful of sand.

"Your brothers don't get any less weird the more I see of them." She lifted the jewelry boxes. "The gifts were a nice touch, though. Completely unexpected."

Azrael chuckled. "The gifts took me by surprise as well." They'd done more than surprise him; they'd given him a fragment of hope that his brothers might accept Sara into their world. He drew her back into his arms. "Let's forget about them and focus on us."

She smiled. "We're married."

"Indeed we are."

"Does that make me Mrs. Death?" She laughed, then sighed and rested her cheek against his chest. "I don't want this feeling to end."

"What feeling is that?"

"This unending happiness. It's like being intoxicated without any of the bad side affects." She exhaled softly. "I don't want to go back to my regular life."

He pulled away to look at her. From this angle, the succulent valley between her breasts begged for his tongue. "What do you mean, your regular life?"

"Work and all that." She waved her hand as if what she spoke of was insignificant.

"Surely you don't think you need to continue working. Everything you need I can take care of."

She patted his chest like he was a child. "I know that, but you can't expect me to just up and quit. I have to give them two weeks notice. It wouldn't be right not to."

"Two weeks?" It seemed an eternity.

"Yes. Two weeks. Now stop pouting and take me back to the room. I want to see what married sex feels like."

"I wasn't pouting, I — okay, let's go." He wasn't about to waste time arguing. Not when she'd end up doing what she wanted anyway. Stubborn mortal woman. He laughed. His stubborn mortal wife.

"What's so funny?" She squeezed his hand as they headed for the elevators.

"Nothing, wife. Nothing at all."

* * *

Sara laid in her bed, in her apartment, Azrael by her side. The weekend had left her pleasantly sore and a little worn out, but she was still sorry it was over. She couldn't bear to open her eyes. Not yet.

She winced. The first pointed fingers of a migraine jabbed into her skull.

He nibbled the curve of her neck. "Are you awake?"

"Almost," she mumbled, rolling away from him to hide a grimace of pain. "I need coffee. I think I had too much champagne again."

He massaged her back. She moaned as the pleasure of his touch warred with the pain blossoming in her head.

"Does that feel good?" he asked.

"Oh, yeah." She didn't want to interrupt him to get coffee, but her system screamed for the caffeine it knew was hot and waiting in the kitchen.

His gentle hands went lower, kneading her shoulder blades then down along her spine. She congratulated herself on marrying so well. Married. She smiled and sighed into her pillow.

He scooped her close against his warm, naked body. "Good morning, wife." He kissed her temple. It began to throb. "Stay in bed. I'll get you some coffee."

"I love you," she whispered. Anything louder would kill her.

The bed moved as he got up. She almost opened her eyes just to watch him walk away. A backside like that should be admired whenever possible. But the thought of letting daylight behind her lids made her nauseous.

She lay there, trying to find the strength to get up and get moving without letting Azrael know how much pain she was in. She didn't want him to worry about something as silly as a headache.

"Here's your coffee, sweetheart." The mattress sunk down as he sat.

She inhaled the fresh brewed aroma and steeled herself. Now or never. She opened her eyes a slit, blinking to clear the haze.

Two Azraels holding two cups of coffee sat beside her. She blinked again but the double vision didn't go away. She rubbed her eyes. It didn't help.

She pushed herself up and a fresh blade of pain cut through her brain. "Oh...ow." She clutched her head, unable to pretend any longer she was fine.

"Sara, what's wrong?"

"Just a headache," she mumbled, drawing her legs up and pressing her forehead into her knees. "I get these migraines every once in a while. It'll pass. They always do." Coffee. What she need was coffee.

She lifted her head, still holding a hand to her brow. "Don't worry, I'll be fine." With a forced smile, she reached for the cup he still held, fighting the double vision to find the real one. Her nose started to run. Great. Coming down with a cold was exactly what she needed.

Azrael's eyes rounded. He set the coffee down before she could take it. "Something's wrong."

"It will be if you don't let me have my coffee." She swiped at her nose and made a mental note to buy tissues. "I get these all the time. I'm fine, I promise."

"No, you're not." He grabbed her hand and held it up so she could see.

A streak of blood smeared her skin. She inhaled, tugged her hand away and wiped at her nose again. More blood. She struggled to stay upright, her ears ringing with a tinny buzz that shut out all other sound. "I don't..."

Her vision narrowed down to pinpoints.

Then everything went black.

Chapter Nineteen

Azrael pounded on the emergency room desk. "What's going on? What's wrong with her? I want to know. I'm her husband."

"Sir, please." The nurse gave him a stern look that did nothing to intimidate him. "The doctors have to run some tests. We'll let you know as soon as they find something out."

"When will that be?" He'd waited hours already.

"I don't know, sir. Could be any time now." She pointed back into the waiting room. "Have a seat and I'll call you as soon as the results come in."

Have a seat. How was he supposed to wait patiently while Sara suffered? Why couldn't he be with her? At least he could hold her hand and tell her everything would be all right. He closed his eyes for a moment, weary of being mortal and powerless. Maybe he should change into Reaper form and slip back there. See for himself what was going on.

A doctor pushed through the swinging doors leading into the patient area. He read some paperwork on a chart, flipping pages as he walked. He stopped at the desk, looked at the nurse. "Page Mr. Grimm."

Azrael stepped forward. "I'm Mr. Grimm."

"I'm Dr. Stein. Why don't we take a walk down to one of the consultation areas and I'll explain what's going on with your wife." The doctor's face was emotionless, his eyes blank. Completely unreadable.

"Fine." He followed the doctor a short way down the hall and into the private room.

Shutting the door, Dr. Stein pointed to one of the chairs. "Would you like to sit?"

"Just tell me what's going on." He fisted his hands at his sides to keep from pummeling the information out of the man. That would help nothing.

Dr. Stein flipped some more papers. "Based on the symptoms your wife was having, we did a series of tests, a chest x-ray, a head CT, an MRI, some blood work." He sighed. "She's got a non small cell carcinoma on her right lung."

"Cancer?" Azrael shook his head. "But that doesn't make sense. That wouldn't give her headaches."

Dr. Stein nodded. "You're right." He tucked the chart under his arm. "We also found a metastatic brain tumor.

That's what caused the headaches, the double vision and the nose bleed."

"What?" Sharp pain punctured Azrael's gut. He couldn't breathe, couldn't see, couldn't think. A cold, fluid numbness leaked down his spine.

He fell into the closest chair. "You can treat this, right?"

The doctor took the chair across from him. "Non small cell carcinomas grow slowly and unlike other types of lung cancer, we can usually remove this with surgery." He paused. "The brain tumor is another story. We'll operate to remove what we can, but its position makes it difficult to get all of it. Radiation and chemo are her best hope."

Azrael sat frozen, trying to find a way to comprehend everything the doctor was telling him. "Can I see her?"

"Not yet, we've still got some more tests to run. Need to make sure the cancer hasn't spread elsewhere. I assure you, she's in good hands and in very little pain right now. We've got her on Mannitol to reduce the brain swelling, which will alleviate some of the headaches."

Azrael spoke around the lump in his throat. "What...what caused this?"

He shrugged. "We're not sure. She's in great physical shape, healthy, non-smoker, much younger than the typical patient who presents with this. Cancer is one of those things where you can't always pinpoint a cause." He sat back. "It's like something flipped a switch in her system that turned the cancer on. Judging from the size of the tumors, it happened pretty recently too."

Azrael buried his face in his hands. He had a good idea what that something was.

* * *

The first fat drops of hard rain hit the Fates' balcony the second after Azrael materialized. The drops drove down, stinging his skin and melding into a solid sheet of water. If this was their way of getting rid of him, they were going to have to try harder.

Much harder.

"Atropos!" He called out with a voice fueled by the Darkness. "Klotho! Lachesis!"

Nothing. Not a curtain moved in the massive stone house. They were in there, he could feel them. Sense them, just as he could his brothers, although not quite as strongly.

"Come out now or I come in."

The rain dribbled to a halt. A few rays of sun leaked through, sparkling off the puddles left behind. One of the balcony doors opened a fraction. Klotho peeked her head out.

"Please, Azrael, go home. We know she's ill, but there's nothing—"

"Don't lie. It spoils your beauty." He unfurled his wings to the sun, casting the Virgin in shadow. "I want an audience with Atropos. Now."

"She doesn't wish to speak to you." Klotho blinked hard.

"And you think what Atropos wishes matters to me?" He opened himself further to the Darkness. Let them see the being he truly was. Let them understand he was done being their pawn. "Send her out."

Klotho shook her head, sadness evident in her limpid blue eyes. "Go home, Azrael."

She moved back to shut the door.

"I will not be dismissed." He gave the Darkness full voice and shouted for Atropos again. Tiny cracks shot through the glass in the first floor windows. Klotho disappeared, quickly replaced by Lachesis.

The Mother waved her silver rod. "What's done is done. Leave us be."

"Send. Atropos. Out." He thrust his wings forward, hurling a blast of wind against the house and shattering the cracked windows.

Lachesis opened her mouth to speak, but a wizened hand on her arm stopped her. Atropos, leaning heavily on her carved-bone cane, shuffled out of the house.

"What do you want, Reaper? I'm weary and need my rest."

"I want answers." The Darkness struggled against his control, but he stayed it for the moment.

"Your mortal is sick. It appears you are to blame. What other answers are there?"

With a gut-deep bellow, he cracked the glass the next story up. "Did I or did I not cause the cancer in her body?"

Atropos cocked her head, her rheumy eyes pinning him with a cold glare. "You fault your brothers for their brief liaisons, but none of their women have grown ill. You chose to spend time with her, to bring her to your home, to couple with her repeatedly..." She shook her gray head, the small hairs on her chin trembling. "One might do well to assume you are to blame."

He howled in frustration.

She spat on the ground. "You are a Reaper. Or have you forgotten that? Death and mortals may mix on occasion, but to create a union with one...pah."

"Blast you, old woman! You encouraged me to pursue her."

"But not to make her part of your life." She sighed. "You are the most foolish of your brothers."

White-hot anger threatened to blind him and wrench away the last bit of control holding back the Darkness. For Sara's sake, he found a sliver of calm and held on a little longer. "Tell me how to fix this."

Atropos smirked. "You're too weak."

For Sara, he would endure anything. "I will do whatever it takes."

"I doubt it."

"Try me."

She dug into the folds of her long robes, extracted a small vial of greenish liquid and tossed it to him.

He caught it and held it up to the light. Bands of black swirled within the mossy depths. "What is this?"

"Give it to her and it will remove all trace of you from her memory. You'll have a few moments once she ingests it to remove yourself from her sight. Then you must never see her again."

He squeezed the bottle in his fist. "How is that going to help?"

"Without the presence of Death in her life, she should be able to recover."

"Should isn't good enough."

Atropos shrugged. "Then stay with her. Sit at her side. Hold her hand. But when she dies before her time and Kol reaps her soul, you will forever wonder if things could have gone differently. Or..." She shrugged.

"Or what?"

She shuffled closer. "Take her soul now, yourself, and spend the rest of your existence peering into the blank eyes of each passing Shade trying to find her."

Disbelief numbed him into silence.

She turned to make her way back inside. "Just as I suspected. You're too weak."

A jagged tear opened across his heart. The pain gave him voice. "How long do I have to say good bye once she takes the potion?"

"A minute or two. Not long."

"And what of her friends? Co-workers? She was registered in the hospital as married. There will be questions." He held the vial up on the tips of his fingers as his insides went numb with sorrow. "I doubt this can solve all that."

Atropos shook her head, leaning heavily on her cane. "A few strands respun, a thread added here or there. We will take care of the rest."

"Then take care of her as well. Don't make me do this."

"You are too deeply threaded through her life." Atropos shuffled toward the door with a long sigh. "Love tangles everything."

* * *

In an empty hospital bathroom, Azrael assumed human form for the last time. There would be little need for it after tonight. He'd already been to Sara's apartment to collect the diamonds he'd bought her and the pearls his

241

brothers had given her. This was the last step. The last time he'd see her. Kiss her. Inhale her scent.

Closing his eyes, he bowed his head, breathing deeply to find a place inside him capable of seeing this wretched but necessary deed through to its end. He'd made her sick. It was his responsibility to give her a chance to get well.

He walked into the hospital's florist shop. Despite the fact he was to leave nothing behind that might remind Sara of him, he refused to go to her bedside empty-handed.

"I'll take those." He pointed to the large bouquet of red roses in the display case.

"Those are awesome. Two dozen definitely says get well better than one." Snapping her gum, the sales girl lifted the vase out and set it on the counter. "Would you like us to deliver them to the room? It's totally free."

He handed her some cash. "No, I'll take them with me."

She gave him his change. "There are little cards right down in front of the register if you'd like to add a note." She pointed with one glittery, black fingernail.

After a moment he selected one, jotted a brief message, then slipped it into an envelope and handed it to the girl.

She secured it into a little plastic holder and stuck it amid the roses. "All set. You must be going to see someone special."

"Yes," he said. His gut knotted. "My wife."

"That's cool. Did she have a baby? We just got these really cute balloons in with baby booties on them and pink—"

"No." The knot pulled tighter. "She has cancer."

"Oh." Her kohl-rimmed eyes widened. "I'm totally sorry."

Ignoring her, he took the roses, made his way into the elevator and up to Sara's floor. How fitting they should say goodbye in the same place they met. His footsteps rang hollow in the quiet hall. Visiting hours would be over soon. The glass vial shifted in his pocket.

He paused at the door to Sara's room. A ravenous ache gnawed his heart raw, shredding the edges into a bloody pulp. He imagined if he had a soul, the pain of what he was about to do would rend it in two. He closed his eyes, inhaled the sour hospital air and opened the door.

The bed made her look small and fragile. The tubes running out of her didn't help. Passing the other empty bed, he went to her side, each step hot coals and broken glass. The window ledge held a potted plant and a pink rabbit holding balloons. It was good to know there were others to care for her when he was gone. He added the roses to the collection and returned to her.

"Sara," he whispered her name, half hoping she would stay asleep and he'd be unable to give her the potion. "It's me, Sara. I'm here."

Her lids fluttered open. Bruised shadows hung beneath her glassy eyes.

"Hi," she whispered back. Her hand went to her throat. "So dry."

He hurried to pour water into the plastic cup provided, sloshing some onto the bedside tray. "Sorry."

She smiled weakly. "S'okay."

He helped her sit, supporting her with an arm behind her back. She felt thin beneath the hospital gown. He kissed her head. Cursed the cancer. Himself.

She sipped then nodded she was done. "Thanks.

He eased her back into the bed. "I'm so sorry..." He griped the bed rail, unable to finish.

She patted his hand. "Az, these things happen."

"Not in this case." He hated himself.

Her face scrunched in a sweet, uncertain expression. "What's that mean?"

"You have... The reason..." He smacked the bed rail and spun away, the dull thunk ringing over the whirr of machines. "I'm the reason you have cancer."

"That's silly. You can't catch cancer." Her hand tugged at his elbow.

He turned back to face her. "You have cancer because of who I am. Because of being around me."

Her mouth opened but nothing came out. Confusion spun through her beautiful eyes.

Leaning over her, he bent down to kiss her forehead, then thought better of it. He'd done enough damage. He stood up, tried to smile for her sake. "Because I am Death, you have begun to die."

She started to shake her head.

"It's true. I'm responsible. But I have this." He fished the wretched glass vial from his pocket. "This..." He tossed the container into the air, catching it with a lightness he didn't feel. "Will make things better."

What else could he tell her? The truth? She would fight it. He knew that much about the woman he'd married. She would never willingly give up being his. His love for her expanded with that thought and his jaw quivered. He ground his teeth together and blinked back the heat building in his eyes. No matter that he was losing the only love he'd ever known. He had to stay strong. For her.

"What is it?"

"Magic." He forced a smile. "To make all your troubles go away." Not a lie.

A lopsided grin lifted one corner of her mouth. "And then I'll be the queen again?"

He swallowed, tried to fight back the guilt buffeting his heart. "You'll always be a queen to me."

He started to thumb the cork off, then stopped. Cancer be damned, he needed to kiss her one last time. He bent and found her mouth. Tenderly, he kissed her and hoped the memory would last an eternity.

Her hand came up to catch his neck. "I love you, Az. And no matter what happens, I don't regret any of this. I wouldn't change a thing."

Her words almost broke him. He bent his head into her chest, felt her kiss the top of his head. Picturing Atropos, he used his anger as a focus. Sara deserved a chance at life.

Purpose renewed, he stood, uncorked the vial and handed it to Sara.

"Here goes nothing." She tipped it to her lips and drank. Grimacing, she handed the empty vial back. "It must be magic, it tastes horrible."

He dropped the container into his pocket.

"I feel funny..." Her lids shuttered, her head lolled to one side.

Lifting her hand, he kissed her knuckle to distract her as he slid her wedding rings off. He pocketed the rings. The soft clink of them against the glass vial jabbed more pain into his heart.

Her lashes fanned over her pale cheeks and her breathing evened out. He slipped his hands behind her neck, found the clasp of the necklace he'd given her on their first date.

"What...are you..." Her head rolled to the other side. "Az...love you."

He unhooked the necklace and squeezed it in his palm, trying to hold onto the heat left in the metal. "I love you, too, Sara. I always will."

Her eyes closed. It was time for him to leave. The pendant went cold in his hand, but the chill was nothing compared to the ice gripping his heart.

Chapter Twenty

A gentle hand shook Sara awake. Manda's kind brown eyes smiled down at her. "Sorry to wake you, baby girl, but I've got to take your temperature."

"Huh?" Sara scrubbed a limp hand over her face. "What?"

"I need to take your temp." Manda slipped the thermometer into Sara's mouth. "Here we go."

"Hmmkay." The pain in her head was the lightest it had been for a long while, but a thick fuzziness had taken its place. She blinked. Tasted the plastic wrapper on the thermometer with her sandpaper tongue.

Manda bustled around the room, doing whatever it was she did. The thermometer beeped. She took it from Sara and read the result. "Slight temp, but that's normal. You're doing great. Can I get you anything?"

"Water." Her hand went to her throat. For a brief moment, her bare neck felt odd. Like there should have been something there. She ignored the sensation. She didn't wear a necklace. Never had.

Manda poured water into a glass, found a straw and helped Sara up. "Here you go."

Sara drank deeply. Water had never tasted so good. "Thanks. That's better." She licked her lips, running her tongue over the chapped skin.

"How's your pain? Don't be brave. If you hurt, hit the button." Manda pressed the controller for the pain meds into her hand.

"I'm okay." Ignoring the controller, she stared at the IV in the back of her hand. She groaned softly. "I can't believe this is happening to me. Like my life isn't crappy enough."

"Honey, cancer doesn't care who you are or what your life is like. It goes after everyone equally. Now it's your job to fight this thing."

"Yeah, I know." She exhaled a long slow sigh. "Have I been out a long time? I feel completely out of it."

"Considering all the meds in your system, that's understandable." Manda wrote a few things in Sara's chart. "Sorry I can't bring you dinner, but you've got surgery first thing tomorrow and you know the drill."

"Yeah." Sara stared at the ceiling. Unwelcome tears blurred her vision.

Manda squeezed her hand. "I know you're scared, sweetheart, but we're all here for you. You're going be fine, you'll see. You're young and strong and this is not going to get the best of you. You survived being married to Ray, didn't you?"

She sniffed and laughed, a few stray tears slipping down her cheeks. "Thanks. I'm really glad I have you guys to look after me." *Married.* Wasn't there something else she ought to know about that? The fog didn't clear in time to make sense of the brief flicker of thought.

"It's going to be all right, you'll see." Manda patted her hand. "Try to sleep, okay?"

"I don't think I can." The dangers of surgery spun through the clouds in her mind. Complications and risks were very possible. She knew that well enough from working on this floor.

Manda picked up the remote and turned on the television. "Maybe there's a movie on. Something to take your mind off things."

Like the nagging feeling that she was supposed to remember something and couldn't.

Dane came in carrying a stuffed bear with a red and white polka dot bow around its neck. "How you doing, kid?" He wiggled the bear's paw in a wave. "Just a little something to cheer you up. Guess I'll put it with the others."

"No, wait." She reached out for the stuffed animal, oddly desperate for something to fill her hands. "He's cute. I want to hold him." Dane handed her the bear and she hugged it close. "Thanks."

"You're welcome." He hitched his thumb toward the line of plants, flowers and stuffed animals on the window ledge. "This place'll be a florist shop in no time."

She tried to think who might have sent her those things, but her mind came up blank. "Could you read some of those cards to me? I can't remember who sent what."

"Sure." He picked up the stuffed bunny. "This is from the crew at Grounded. They say get well soon, coffee sales are way down."

She smiled. "Keysha definitely wrote that."

He moved on the basket of assorted potted plants. "This one's from your brother and mother, but there's not much on the card besides get well and we love you."

"How do they know I'm in here?" She glanced at Manda.

"One of them must be listed as your next of kin. I'm sure registration called," Manda said.

Dane continued to a colorful mixed bouquet. "This one is from all of us on the floor. We all signed the card."

"Except Charlene," Manda said. "She's been out with the flu for two days."

Beside the mixed bouquet was a huge arrangement of roses. Dane twisted the vase to reach the card. "This one's not open yet. Want me to leave it?"

"No, open it. They're probably from Ray trying to make himself look good." She snorted. "Like I don't know he's already thinking if I die, he doesn't have to pay alimony anymore."

Face stern, Manda lightly smacked her leg. "Don't even say things like that."

Sara laughed. "You know it's true."

Dane ripped the envelope open and pulled out the small florist card. He scanned it, then looked up with an odd glint in his eyes. He smiled and shook his head. "I don't think this is from Ray."

"Why not?" Sara asked.

"'Cause I doubt Ray would write this." He handed her the card.

A line of small, artsy hearts bordered the card and an easy, loping gait defined a handwriting that looked vaguely familiar. She read the message. Dane was right, the words wouldn't have come from Ray.

Manda nudged her. "What's it say?"

She looked up. *"You'll always have my heart."*

Manda laughed. "Yeah, if Ray sent them, it'd probably say you'll always have my wallet."

Dean chuckled along with her. "Sounds like you have a secret admirer."

"Or a weird stalker who picks on cancer patients." Sara turned the card over but there was no signature. "Let me see the envelope?"

Dane handed it over. Blank except for the florist's shop name and address. She pointed it at the roses. "At least we know they came from the shop here."

Manda checked her watch. "They're open another hour. You want to have Dane call down, see if he can find out who sent them?"

"Why me?" Dane asked. "I have work to do too, you know."

"You're off in forty-five minutes." Manda stuck her ample chest out and crossed her arms beneath it. "Plus I'm the boss and everybody knows you could charm the habit off a nun."

He grinned. "Can't argue that."

Manda looked at Sara. "So what do you think?"

She drew her shoulders up. "Yeah, I guess. Might as well." She smiled despite the feeling of certainty that Dane wouldn't find anything. The smile suddenly faded. "You know, they were probably delivered to me by mistake."

"I doubt that," Manda said. "Those meds are just playing with your head. You'll figure out who sent them soon enough. Probably some hot guy you've been keeping a secret." She winked.

Sara sighed. Her memory loss was most likely a combined side effect of the tumor and the meds, but that didn't make the blanks in her memory any less disturbing. Nor did it explain the overwhelming sense of melancholy that reminded her of one other particular emotion. One very similar to what she'd gone through during the divorce.

She couldn't really say why, but she felt like she'd been dumped.

* * *

Vitus extended the silver tray bearing Azrael's dinner a second time.

"I told you I'm not hungry." And he hadn't been since he'd left Sara's hospital room. He rolled her wedding ring in his fingers. Keeping it warm helped him pretend she'd just taken it off, that she was close by. But pretending couldn't fill the gaping hole inside him. Not even the two separate occasions when Chronos and Kol had come to visit. Admittedly, the visits had been quite a surprise until he realized they'd probably come to remind him they'd been right about his involvement with Sara. Not letting them in had been a wise decision.

Vitus still stood over him.

"What?"

The Shade's brows drew together. He notched his head to one side and stared his master down, urging the tray forward a third time.

"Enough. You can't guilt me into eating." Azrael slumped back into the leather chair, his gaze focused on the world beyond his windows. He saw nothing but a future of misery.

"Maybe I'll get lucky and starve to death," he mumbled, knowing the impossibility of his words even as they left his mouth. He rolled Sara's engagement ring in his fingers, staring at the sparkling diamond that had brought such a huge smile to her face.

Why had he succumbed to the Fates' wishes and given her that vial? He slipped the ring onto his pinky. What if he'd stayed away long enough for her to get well, then explained he could only see her once in awhile? A hard sigh hissed from his mouth. He could no more stay away from her than he could stop reaping souls.

Leaning his elbows on the chair's arms, he cradled his head in his hands and wished for a soul so that he could die and end the tremors of longing that racked every bone in his body. Every sensation brought Sara to mind. Even reaping souls, the work that had once brought him a sense of place and purpose, irritated him due to the necessary trip to the Fates to gather the allotted threads.

Then there were the past days and nights – how many, he didn't know because time had lost meaning – he'd spent wandering the grounds of his home, studying the passing Shades to see if he could distinguish one from another.

He couldn't.

Not only had he lost Sara, but if she didn't recover and ended up passing into his world some other way, he'd have no way of finding her once she became a Shade. His only chance was that she'd find him and discover a way to make him understand who she was.

Unless the Fate's potion extended beyond the grave and even her Shade form had no memory of him. The thought severed the few remaining strands of hope he'd been clinging to. His heart plummeted.

"No!" He jumped from the chair, knocking it to the floor with a loud thud. Vitus, who now stood empty-handed by the great room door, didn't budge. Azrael tucked her ring back into his pocket for safe keeping, then grabbed the chair, lifted it overhead and aimed it at the windows he'd just been looking out. The need to destroy something surged hot in his veins.

Vitus was instantly in front of him, shaking his head.

"Get out of my way. This is my home, I'll do what I—"

Vitus reached into his pocket, retrieved something and held out his clenched fist.

Azrael held the chair ready, his muscles clenched and ready. "What?"

Vitus opened his hand. In his palm lay his own life thread, returned to him when he'd come into Azrael's service as a promise from the Fates his life would never be tampered with again.

Azrael set the chair down and stared for a moment without understanding.

Vitus thrust his open hand out again, using his other to jab a finger down on the thread repeatedly. His mouth strained, his eyes wide.

Realization smacked Azrael. He nodded, did his best to breath evenly. Amazing how astute a Shade could be when given a chance.

"Vitus, my friend, you're absolutely right."

* * *

Intense pain wrapped a band around Sara's head, but the rest of her body floated. Or drowned. She couldn't tell. Moaning softly, she opened her eyes a slit.

Fuzzy starbursts sprouted from the dimmed lights overhead. She blinked a few times, but they didn't budge. Her teeth chattered and her entire body began to shake.

She was freezing. Arctic cold.

"You're awake. Good, good. Don't try to move. You're in recovery. How's your pain?"

257

The voice belonged to Linda, one of the day nurses, but Sara couldn't see her from her position in the bed. Her teeth started to chatter and shivers ran through her body.

"Being cold is a normal reaction. You're coming out of anesthesia. I'll get you another blanket."

She tried to sit up, but a wave of dizziness swept her. She collapsed back down onto the bed as Linda returned.

Linda tossed the new blanket over her, tucking it in around her legs. "It's okay, honey, you're in recovery. Just rest now. No need to get up."

Still shivering uncontrollably, she moved again, just wiggling her toes this time to be sure she could. She opened her mouth to speak. Nothing came out. Her tongue was a useless piece of cotton. She tried again.

"D-dry."

The single word was the best she could manage through the fog of pain and meds. Linda came into view above her, holding a cup with a bendy straw.

"I bet you are. Let's get some water into you, okay?" She lowered the cup and guided the straw to Sara's mouth. "Slow now. Don't want you getting sick."

Tepid water splashed down her throat, bringing relief in a wet rush. Nothing compared to how good the first sip tasted, not coffee, not coffee chocolate chip ice cream, nothing. She drank until she'd emptied the cup, her teeth creasing the straw as they clenched reflexively from the unshakable chill.

"Thanks. More?" she asked.

"I'll bring you more in a little bit. Too much and you could get nauseous," Linda said, patting her arm. "Now, how's your pain level?"

"S-seven. Six." After managing her headaches for so long, the pain was something she could deal with. She struggled to break the mental ropes left behind by the anesthesia and put voice to the question in her head. "When will I be out of here?" The words tasted like clods of dirt, even after the water.

Linda rested her hand on Sara's arm. "You'll be on your back for four or five days until some real healing begins. The best they could do was debulk the tumor, so now it's up to radiation to get the rest."

"Radiation?" She hadn't expected that. She'd thought the surgery would be the worst of it, but then, she should that would be the result if they couldn't remove the tumor in its entirety. A wave of self-pity washed through her. She shoved it back, determined to fight. "I want...a mirror."

"You said your pain was a six, so let me get you some Demerol and I'll be right—"

"A mirror."

"I don't think right after surgery would be the best time. You really don't want to—"

"Yes, I do." She wanted to see what was left of her hair. It hadn't been that great to begin with. She shoved away another bout of pity. Not like the chemo wouldn't cause her to lose it all anyway. She stared at the ceiling, listening to Linda's footsteps fade away, then return.

Maybe her hair would grow back blonde and curly. That seemed a small repayment for this misery.

Linda returned, syringe in hand. She fished for the IV port. "The doctor will be in soon. How about you let him explain things better and we'll go from there."

"I'm going to see..." The warm flush of Demerol rolled over her like a weighty down comforter. At last, her shivering stopped. "...sooner or...later."

"Later it is then." Linda's footsteps faded away.

The lights went off and Sara drifted back into the dark, weightless void she'd just escaped.

Chapter Twenty-One

Azrael hovered halfway between his visceral and Reaper forms above the stone balcony. In response to his mood, an artificial twilight had begun to silence the ever-present songbirds and cloak the perpetually blue sky.

Vitus was right. Destroying his own home was a poor decision. Especially when the Fates were the ones behind everything that had gone wrong. In the distance, thunder rumbled low and menacing.

Let them lose something precious. Find a way to rebuild life as it had been. He growled deep in his throat and thrust out his arms. Wind whipped through the tattered shadows of his form. He wrapped tendrils of control further around the foundation of the house. This storm would be unlike any the Fates had experienced before, of that much he was sure.

Clean lines of thought blurred as his visceral self took over. Foremost was Sara's image, but sweeping past came tactile memories of her warmth pressed against him on

Pallidus' back, the softness of her lips on his, the sweet scent of her hair, the way their bodies fit, the hushed, fevered moans that had escaped her as they made love.

A low keening yowl ripped out of him. Lightning arced from the black clouds, cracking the balcony and leaving behind a charred chasm.

The doors flew open. Atropos, hair blowing wild around her leathery face, stood braced with her cane, one gnarled fist lifted. "You will stop this immediately! Go back to your world and leave us to ours."

He shook his head. The Crone was most responsible of all, so she should be made to pay the most. It was only fair. He regained a small portion of control, enough to give voice and body to his rage. "You meddled in my world. Now I meddle in yours."

Maintaining some of his Reaper form, he brandished his scythe in his right hand. The tool extended to its full size in a blinding glint of silver.

Her eyes rounded, but she held her ground. "It is our calling to set the paths of mortals."

He hefted the scythe. Tested its comfortable weight. The tool came alive in his hands. Hummed with power. Soothed him. But not enough. Nothing would ever be enough again.

"Then you overstepped your bounds, Crone. I am not mortal. My path is mine to set."

Swinging the scythe, he sliced cleanly through the limestone header above the door, sending a shower of dust and debris onto her old head. The clouds split as well. Rain poured down in tiny daggers.

Atropos wrapped her arms around her frail body. Klotho and Lachesis huddled behind her, strands of wet hair clinging to their cheeks. They tugged at Atropos, obviously imploring her to do something. She shook them off. "You'll pay for this, Reaper," she called through the howling wind.

He tipped his head back and laughed. "I already have. And now I have nothing to lose."

Unfurling his wings farther, he snapped them forward, buffeting the house with more wind and shattering the newly replaced windows once again.

He arched his wings back for another blow, hoping this time to bring down a wall.

"Please, Azrael, don't!" Klotho cried, darting out to stand in front of Atropos and Lachesis. Tears mixed with the rain on her face. "You must understand this is the way of things."

"Why?" he snapped. "Why must I understand the pain and hurt you've caused?"

A second bolt of lightning shattered a huge section of the balcony, shearing a portion off and dropping it into the valley below with a tremendous crash. Klotho clutched at Azrael, but her fingers slipped through the vaporous strands of his robe, unable to touch him. "Please, stop it! You're destroying our home."

"You destroyed Sara's life. My life. Our hope for a future." Pulling his wings in, he nodded toward the crumbling limestone. "This hardly seems an equal trade, but it will suffice for now."

"Please," she begged, "there must be something else..."

"Bring Sara back to me."

"No," Atropos spat. "It cannot be done."

"Then there is nothing left to discuss." He spread his wings again.

"What if you could see her? Just for a few minutes?" Klotho wrung her hands.

"Klotho, no." Lachesis shook her head but kept her eyes on him. "She may still be able to see him. "

A pinpoint of hope opened up in his heart. "For a few minutes with Sara, I would spare your home."

Atropos hobbled forward to jab her cane into Klotho's hip. She yelped in pain and ran back to Lachesis. Atropos's acid gaze followed her. "Foolish girl. You should learn to keep your mouth shut."

She turned her rheumy eyes on him. "I won't allow it. As I said before, you're too weak. Once you see her, you will want more and there is no more to give."

Fresh anger boiled through his gut. He bent toward the old woman and met her with a gaze that would have seared her bones, had he been Kol. "I. Am. Not. Weak." He punctuated the words with a sharp peal of thunder. "I gave her your potion. I did exactly as you asked. I have *always* done exactly as you asked." Barely an inch separated his nose from the tip of the Crone's. "I demand this of you."

Her sudden, toothless grin rocked him back a pace. "You demand it of me? You are too bold by half."

"Please, Atropos," Klotho begged.

"He is too weak, but what do I care?" Shaking her head, the Crone raised her clenched fist. A pale, twisted thread dangled from her fingers, pulled sideways by the stormy gusts.

The wind died, and the rain ceased. "Is that—"

"No. Not her's." She thrust her veiny hand toward him. "But it will take you where you want to go."

He snatched the thread before she could take it back. Instantly, everything he needed to know about the next soul to be reaped flooded his consciousness. The soul would be ready to harvest in one day's time.

She raised one bony finger. "Be warned. You can undo all that has been done, but it will not be as it was."

Taking his full Reaper form, he tucked the thread deep into the pocket of his robe. "Save your riddles for someone who cares, old woman. I have work to do."

And a wife to save.

* * *

Sara pressed her lips together as firmly as she could. Manda nudged them again with the spoonful of applesauce.

"Open up. You need to eat."

Sara grunted a "no" as best she could through a closed mouth.

Manda dropped the spoon back onto the tray. "Obviously, the stubborn part of your brain has been completely unaffected by all of this."

Feeling certain Manda's retreat was permanent, Sara spoke. "I have no appetite. And anything I do eat comes right back up thanks to these meds and the radiation."

Manda's eyes softened. "I know, baby girl, I know. Just a few more treatments."

"Yeah, if I live that long."

"Come on, now." She patted Sara's hand. "You're doing great."

"Great my –"

"Anybody up for a sponge bath?" Dane's familiar laugh followed his offer as he entered. He leaned over so Sara could see him better. "How you doing?"

"How do you think I'm doing?"

Manda sighed. "She's cranky and won't eat. What's new?"

"I'm still the most handsome nurse on day shift. Wait, that's not new." He laughed and waved a romance novel. "I'm off in half an hour. Want me read to you some more?"

"No. That happily ever after crap is such a lie. How come no one in those books ever gets brain cancer? Because it's not warm and fuzzy, that's why." The bed creaked softly from her shifting. She huffed out a breath. "Sorry. You'd be cranky too in my position. If it weren't for work friends, I'd have no visitors at all."

Manda tapped the bed rail with a burgundy-polished nail. "So you're not counting Ray?"

She rolled her gaze up to stare at the ceiling. "That vulture? I don't count him coming by to see if I'm still warm as a visit."

Dane whistled. "You probably don't want to hear what I have to tell you about those roses then."

Sara punched the button to raise her bed the few inches she was allowed, slanting her eyes in his direction until she inclined enough to see him. "What?"

Dane frowned. "I finally ran into the girl who worked the night those flowers were bought. Said she can't remember much about the guy except he was good looking and buying the flowers for his wife."

An image flickered in her head, as brief as a lightning flash. Dark eyes flecked with blue. Eyes she knew.

Eyes that knew her.

And then they were gone.

Her hands trembled. She clenched handfuls of blanket to anchor herself. "Ray didn't send them."

"Sure sounds like him," Manda said. "Although why he'd call you his wife is beyond me. Maybe you being sick has got him all sentimental for the good old days."

"We never had any good old days." She shook her head gently. "No, I know they didn't come from him."

Manda raised a brow. "How you know that?"

"I just do." She pursed her lips. "Ray doesn't have dark eyes."

"I knew there was a secret boyfriend." Crossing her arms and shooting a look at Dane, Manda cleared her throat. "What aren't you telling us?"

"I don't know! My memory is full of holes. I can't remember anything clearly anymore." Frustration sharpened the dull pain shrouding her head. She squeezed her eyes shut and growled in disgust. "Oh, forget it. For all I know, I'm remembering someone I saw on TV or something Dane read to me out of that stupid book."

Dane waved the novel again. "Are you sure you don't want to hear more? I think we're like two pages from a major sex scene."

"I'm never having sex again so why should I torture myself?"

"Never?" he asked.

She snorted. "You think some man is going to find this attractive?" She waved her hand at her shaved head.

He shrugged. "I don't know. There's something oddly sexy about the whole Sinead O'Connor thing."

"You're an idiot."

Manda clapped. "That's the truth." She shook her head. "The man is *not* right."

"Hey, I don't see you doing anything to make her feel better."

Planting her hands on her hips, Manda went face to face with Dane. "You listen here—"

"Enough," Sara intervened, holding up her hands. Her plate held plenty without dealing with her friends fighting. "Just leave me alone, okay? I'm not in the mood for company right now."

"See what you did?" Manda hissed at Dane before turning back to Sara. "You best hope your mood changes soon then, 'cause that bed next to you is getting filled tomorrow."

"Fine with me. I doubt whoever you put in here is going to be as chatty as you two." She loved her friends, she really did, but her emotions were grinding her down and there was no one else to take them out on. She swallowed. "I didn't mean to snap, it's just—"

"Hush." Manda stopped her. "Now, don't you worry about it. We all understand what you're going through. And we all know what a gigantic butt pain Dane can be."

"Hey!" Dane said.

Sara smiled. "Thanks for understanding." She hesitated. "I really would like to be left alone for a bit. I just need some time to think. Or try to think."

"You got it. Let's go, Mr. Romance." Manda motioned for Dane to exit ahead of her, then she shut the door, leaving Sara in silence.

She hit the button to lower her bed back down, then stopped as her gaze hung on the large bouquet of roses.

Someone had spent a lot of money on those. The hospital florist shop wasn't known for its bargains. Why couldn't she remember who they'd come from?

Every time she felt like she was close to remembering, the tiny thread of thought slipped away. No matter how hard she tried, she couldn't grab it fast enough. Her head throbbed with the effort. She inhaled and exhaled a few times, trying to clear the pain.

If she ever did remember, it might be the death of her.

Chapter Twenty-Two

Azrael strode down the hall with more purpose in his step than he'd felt in a long while. Just knowing he would see Sara, even for a few moments, renewed his spirit. Despite Atropos's warning, he fully intended on talking to her. He had to. Had to explain his plan, how he'd figured out a way for them to be together, even if it was a little tricky.

When in the course of her lifespan the day came that she passed on from a natural, timely death, he would be there, even if he wasn't the Reaper her soul was assigned to. He'd fight his brothers if necessary. Whatever it took to hold onto her soul, then he would petition the Fates for her to be reborn as a being of his world. A dual being such as himself, who could walk both realms safely.

They could be together forever.

He squeezed the thread in his fist. Just from the feel of it, he knew he drew near to Frances Corbell, the dying mortal whose soul he'd been assigned. Once he reaped her soul, he'd be free to find Sara.

Rounding the corner, he came face to face with Chronos and Kol.

He stopped short. "If you're here to tell me you told me so, forget it. I'm not listening."

"We figured that out when you wouldn't let us into your house, you jackhole," Kol said.

Azrael tamped down his temper. "Then what are you doing here?"

Chronos spoke before Kol could respond. "I went to collect my threads and Lachesis told me what happened."

Azrael sighed. It was no secret how Lachesis felt about Chronos. She'd do anything for him, even though he never did anything to encourage her advances. A dalliance with one of the Fates was asking for trouble. "So?"

Kol stepped forward. "So it's obviously a trap. You think Atropos is just going to let you see Sara again? Why would she do that? Because her heart is overflowing with rainbows and kittens?"

"And you two are here to stop me. I don't think so." Azrael brushed Kol aside and kept moving.

Chronos shot an arm out in front of him. "We're here to warn you and keep you from doing something you'll regret."

"How do you know what I'll regret?" His temper flared. Typical Chronos, always telling him how to live his life.

"I don't know, but I agree with Kol. Atropos is up to something."

"Face it," Kol said. "You trashed her home. She wants revenge."

"Making me give Sara that potion wasn't punishment enough?"

Chronos threw his hands up. "I don't argue that. I only know what Lachesis said."

"Which was?"

A nurse walked through their midst, oblivious to the three Reapers standing in the hospital corridor. Her path took her directly through Chronos. He shook himself as she moved on, tearing three spots in his robe. Spiders swarmed to the repairs. "I hate when mortals do that. You can hear everything they're thinking."

Azrael clenched his fists impatiently. "Can we get back to the matter at hand? What did Lachesis say?"

"That Atropos gave in to you too quickly. That the thread Atropos gave you neither she nor Klotho had seen before."

"Means nothing." Azrael started forward again.

This time Kol's hand stopped him. "We just want you to be careful."

Dumbfounded, he stared at Kol like he'd just announced he was going to work a few shifts at the Salvation Army. "You want me to be careful. You. Since when do you care about me or anything I do?"

"I don't care, it's just..." A deep rumble sounded from Kol's chest. "You're the only bloody family I have, all right?"

Chronos cleared his throat.

Kol punched Chronos in the arm. "Besides you, okay?" He glared through his shades at Azrael. "Stop being such an ass and listen. We're trying to help."

A baby's breath could have knocked Azrael down. He'd never imagined words like that even existed in Kol's vocabulary, never mind that he'd actually say them. Unable to help himself, he smiled.

Kol grimaced and backed up a step. "Wipe that stupid grin off your face. Hug me and I swear I will beat you until not a single feather remains on those pretty boy wings."

Chronos intervened. "What Kol means is that we may not be close like a mortal family, but we do care what happens to you. You're as much a part of us as we are of you. And we don't want you to walk into this situation blind. I'm sure you'd do the same for us." He sighed. "We haven't been the best brothers to you, and we're sorry for it."

Azrael bowed slightly. Chronos' words humbled him, dissipated his remaining anger. "I appreciate your warning, but Atropos's actions don't surprise me. She and I have never had a peaceable relationship. But trap or not, nothing is going to stop me from seeing Sara again. I love her. That's all there is to it."

"Idiot," Kol murmured.

Azrael smiled. "Love does that to you."

"Just be careful, then," Chronos said.

"I will. Thank you for coming. And caring."

"I knew I was going to regret this." Kol rolled his eyes and disappeared.

"You're welcome." Chronos clapped Azrael on the back, then vanished as well.

Shaking his head with amazement, Azrael continued on to the correct room. His wings brushed the doorframe as he entered the room. The soft glow of medical equipment provided enough light to see, although he didn't really need it. He knew the first bed held Frances. He sensed her soul easily.

He shut the door and did a quick check of the room for anything unusual. Anything that might be construed as a trap. Nothing seemed out of place. The mortal in the second bed shifted, but Azrael paid no mind. He had a job to do and his love to visit.

He walked between the beds and was about to put his hands on Frances when she opened her eyes.

She stared up at him, but her face held no fear. "'Bout time you got here," she whispered. "I'm tired of this pain. I'm ready to go and be with my Walter again."

"I know, Frances." He nodded, offering her a comforting smile. Being with the one you loved was all that ever mattered, mortal or otherwise. "You'll be with Walter very soon."

Her lids drooped as his arms went around her. Without further words, he released her soul, offering a silent wish for her and Walter to be reunited as soon as possible, then eased her empty shell back to the bed.

"Az..."

He looked down at Frances. He was certain he'd released her soul. Could this be the trap? Laying his hand on her body, he double-checked. No life. Maybe the sound had come from the machines. No matter, he had to find Sara.

"Az..."

The voice came from behind him, definitely not a machine. He turned around. Maybe Kol was playing a trick on him, trying to make up for his earlier confession. Or trying to make his prediction come true.

A hand reached up from the second bed. "Az." The voice was faint and thready, but familiar.

He went closer, peering through the darkness. The bed held a woman, hair gone from the cancer drugs and being shaved for surgery. Her face was drawn and pale, except for the heavy circles beneath her beautiful brown eyes.

Bile rose in his throat. Sara. What had they done to his beloved?

He reached for her hand, intending to press it to his cheek, then realized that would only cause more damage. He'd never imagined the cancer would leave her like this. He wished now he'd taken the Fates house down to rubble.

"Az...Az..." She blinked, like she was trying to focus. Trying to remember.

He stepped back. This had been a trap. A plan to use his own selfish desires to torture him further. Sara wouldn't recover from this. Because of him, she'd die before her time, become a Shade and be bound to wander forever alone. Atropos had wanted him to see his beloved and understand there was no hope for her.

He had to leave while he still could, before she remembered him and lost any chance she had for a timely, peaceful death.

She deserved that.

He backed away, turning around once he'd passed Frances' bed. His hand reached the knob, its cool metal twisting in his hand.

"Azrael."

Too late.

Chapter Twenty-Three

Sara smiled. She'd finally hung onto a thread long enough to remember something. It felt good. Really good. Even though she wasn't sure what to do with the piece she'd caught.

"Azrael." She said it again, watching the winged man by the door stop and turn around to look at her. Maybe it was his name. She wasn't sure. Pain meds made her so foggy.

He seemed scared. Or worried maybe. She didn't know why. "Azrael." She said it again, just to taste the joy of remembering.

"This is...just a dream," he said.

"That's nice," she answered. "This is a much better dream than the ones I've been having."

He came closer. "Why? What are they like?"

She half-closed her eyes. She was sleepy all the time lately. "Usually something pressing on my head."

She ran a hand over the peach fuzz on her scalp. "I thought maybe in my dream I'd have hair." Wistfulness welled up in her. "I want it to grow back blonde and curly. Wouldn't that pretty?"

"I think straight, brown hair is beautiful." His voice hitched, caught on the last word.

His statement flipped a tiny switch to an even smaller light. "My head hurts."

He swallowed and dropped his gaze to the floor. "I know. I'm sorry."

"Everybody says that, but it's nobody's fault."

"Sara..." He closed his eyes. Was he having trouble breathing?

He knew her name. "Are you an angel?"

"No." He looked up. "Yes. Yes, you're dreaming about an angel."

"That must be how you know who I am." She opened her eyes a little more to see him better. "Can I touch your wings? They look so soft."

He hesitated. Maybe she'd scared him. She should say something nice, to make him feel better.

"Are all angels as handsome as you?"

He smiled, lighting up the flecks of blue in his eyes. Those eyes. And that brilliant, blinding smile. Her head ached with it, but the pain was good and fresh, like a drink of bone-chillingly cold water on a hot, hot day.

Those eyes.

"Azrael." She said it again with new meaning. Sharp memories lanced through her. "You are an angel. The Angel of Death." She struggled to sit up. "Are you here to take me?" She wasn't ready to die. There was something that felt unfinished in her life.

"No, I'm not here to take you." He shook his head, frowning. "This is just a dream." He backed away as if to leave.

"Please, don't go. I'm not scared of you, I know that much." She reached out but he wouldn't take her hand. Every second brought a snippet of her past, but the last flash stunned her. This wasn't just any man. Her jaw fell open and her fingers curled back to point at him.

"You love me." Her hand trembled, but she knew in her bones it was true. "You...you...asked me to marry you."

He rubbed his hand across his face and began nodding slowly.

"And I said yes." Her fingers rose to her mouth. Her heart thudded like it might burst. Another realization, as bright and shining as a newly minted coin, revealed itself. Her hand fell into her lap. "I love you, too."

His eyes filled with longing. "Sara. Sara." He returned to her bed. "I shouldn't be here. You shouldn't be seeing me. This isn't going to help anything. I'm sorry.

I never meant for any of this to happen. I didn't know."
He bent his head. "I didn't know."

"You didn't know what?" The fog in her brain was
still thick in some spots and his words weren't helping.
"What didn't you mean to happen? For us to fall in love?
Why am I in love with the Angel of Death?"

"You weren't supposed to remember." He lifted his
head, his gaze coming to rest on something across the
room. "I shouldn't have left the roses behind."

The roses.

A hot bolt of pain shot through her and she cried out.
Everything came back in one boiling gush that cleared
away all remaining fog.

Meeting him in Edna's room. The ride on Pallidus.
Dinner at her house. Dinner at his. Vegas. The wedding.

The potion.

"You lied to me." She pounded his chest with her
fists. As weak as she was, she doubted he felt much, but
hitting him certainly made her feel better. "You lied to me
and left me to die."

"No, Sara." He caught her hands, brought them to his
mouth and feathered kisses over them. "I left you here to
live."

He explained everything that had happened, holding
her hands all the while.

She nodded. "You're right. I never would have taken that potion if I'd know the truth." She wriggled one hand free and weakly punched his chest again. "That doesn't mean you're forgiven."

"I'm okay with that." He kissed the hand he still held. "I can't stay. The longer I'm here, the worse it is for you. I'm just glad I got to see you one last time. Touch you." He bent and pressed his mouth to hers. "Kiss you."

She reached for him, wound her fingers into his hair. "I love you, and I've missed you, but there's one thing you should know."

"I missed you, too." He kissed her again. "What do I need to know?"

"You're not leaving without me."

"What? No." He pulled away. "I can't."

She held onto him, refusing to let him go again. "Why not? Reap my soul, take me with you."

"You'll be a Shade."

Nothing mattered but being with him and anything was better than being here and going through this misery alone. "I know, but—"

"No." He undid her grip on him and paced to the end of the bed. "I tried to distinguish one Shade from another and I can't. Unless you were able to find a way to communicate with me, which I doubt is possible, you'd be trapped in a horrible limbo." He swung around to face her. "I can't spend the rest of my existence knowing you're out there, but that I can't reach you."

Deflated, she sunk into her pillow. "I want to be with you. That's all I care about."

"I feel the same way, but it has to be done correctly. And I think I have a way...but it will require patience. And cooperation. And you doing your best to recover."

She propped herself up on her elbows. "Tell me."

When he finished, she shook her head. "No. Number one, I don't want to wait that long. Number two..." She collapsed down and twisted the sheet around her hand. "I don't think I'm going to survive this. They couldn't get the entire tumor with surgery, so they went after it with radiation. No dice. I start chemo tomorrow. It doesn't look good. I've worked on this floor long enough to know what the survival rates are for cancer like this."

He leaned against the bed, like he was about to speak. To try to convince her, she was sure. She patted his hand. "And based on recent events, the Fates don't seem all that willing or likely to do nice things for you. Turn me into a Shade and trust me, I'll find you."

"I'm not willing to take that chance."

She sighed and stared at the ceiling. Why did she have to fall in love with a man she'd never get to be with? Anger kept her quiet. She didn't want him to think she was mad at him and have that as his last memory of her. There had to be a way for them to be together.

A nurse came in. Sara lay still as the woman checked Frances' vitals, turned off her machines, then took her chart and left again.

Azrael broke the silence when the nurse had gone. "I should go, Sara. But I'd like to leave you with this." From somewhere in his robe, he retrieved the winged pendant he'd given her on their first date. "It was always meant for you. And now that you remember, there doesn't seem to be a reason for you not to have it."

She opened her hand. He dropped it onto her palm. Curling her fingers around the necklace, she brought her hand to her heart. "Where did you get this?"

He hung his head. "I took it from you, after you took the potion."

"No, I mean where did it come from originally?"

"I created it. For you."

She gave him a wink. "I figured that much. What did you make it from? Pixie dust? Underworld mud?"

"Ah." He nodded in understanding. "From two of my feathers, one from each wing."

"Excellent." She struggled to a sitting position, opened her hand and stared at the pendant. "Would you say this is a piece of you, then?"

"I guess so. Sure." He looked completely befuddled.

Smiling, she lifted the ends of the chain around her neck. "Help me? Even without hair in the way, I still can't hook these things."

He planted a gentle kiss on her bare scalp, then fastened the necklace. Every brush of his fingers against her neck sent warm shivers down her spine.

Fingers twisting in the chain, she lay back down and gazed up at him. "You can reap my soul now."

"We've been over this."

"Yes, but with a piece of you attached to me, I don't see how you can fail to recognize me." She tapped the pendant. "This will make it happen. You'll see."

His eyes lit up. "You might actually have something there."

"I do, trust me." She closed her eyes, then opened them again. "It's not going to hurt, is it?"

"No." He sighed.

She could tell he wasn't entirely on board with the idea. "You're wasting time."

"That's the Sara I know and love." He smiled. "Are you sure about this?"

"Yes. No reservations."

"All right then." He slanted his body over hers, his arms reaching to wrap around her.

"Azrael."

They both turned at the interruption. Chronos stood at the foot of the bed.

"Now is not her time, brother. You'll turn her into a Shade."

Sara clutched the pendant. "I know all that and I'm fine with it. We have a plan."

Putting his hand on her arm, Azrael nodded. "We know what we're doing."

"Do you?" Chronos asked. He held up his silver hourglass. The top globe contained more sand than the bottom. "This is Sara's life."

Azrael's touch went cold. "She survives the cancer?"

"With many years ahead of her."

Azrael stepped away. "I can't do this, Sara. I love you too much to risk this going wrong."

"No! You have to. I want to be with you." Panic rose thick and bitter in her throat. She could not allow Azrael to leave her again.

* * *

"What's going on?" Azrael tipped his chin toward Chronos' hourglass. The sand had sped from a slow trickle to a steady flowing stream. The top globe was fast emptying into the lower one.

Chronos studied the hourglass for a moment, then shook his head. "She's willing herself to die."

"She can do that?"

"Apparently."

Azrael grabbed Sara's shoulders. Her eyes were closed and face screwed into a concentrated mask. "Stop this, Sara. It's madness."

Her eyes flicked open. "Then reap my soul. Take me with you. I won't be left behind again."

Indecision tore at Azrael's heart. He wanted Sara, but not at the cost of her life. He looked back at Chronos. "And if I don't?"

"At this rate, she'll die anyway." Chronos extended the hourglass. The sand grains sparkled softly in the dim light. "You don't have much time."

He growled softly at Sara. "Stubborn woman."

"You married me," she whispered.

"I did, so you should probably have this back, too." He slipped her wedding ring back onto her finger.

She smiled. "Now take me home."

Bracing himself for the worst, he kissed her forehead, wrapped her in his arms and pulled her soul from her body.

Chapter Twenty-Four

Two weeks.

Laying on the bed in the room he'd designed specifically for Sara, Azrael stared blindly at the ceiling of stars.

Two guilt-ridden weeks of searching the fields surrounding his and his brother's homes for the slightest sign of a Shade wearing a winged pendant and a diamond ring.

Nothing. They'd' been fools to think those trinkets would have passed into this realm with her. How could they? He knew better, and yet he'd let her talk him into that ridiculous scheme.

Now his dear, sweet, beautiful Sara was gone. And he had only himself to blame. His foolish, desperate, lovesick self. He pounded his fist into the bed with a growl. His brothers had been right about the hospital being a trap. Once again, the Fates had bested him.

For the second time in his existence, he wished he could die. How lucky mortals were to be able to leave their pain behind. He hoped wherever Sara was, she wasn't suffering in any way. He had enough of that for both of them. Adding to his misery was the fact that his entire staff was missing. As if the Fates hadn't done enough, they'd taken away the only companionship he'd known before Sara.

He cursed Atropos for the millionth time and wished to die again. Or for that biter old Crone to die. A horrible, painful death that would—

"Azrael!" Chronos' voice echoed through the hall outside.

Azrael groaned. No Vitus meant no one to keep his brothers out, either. Despite the fact that they'd professed their concern, he still didn't want company. But he knew if he didn't answer, his brother would just keep yelling. "Leave me alone. Unless you've come to reap my soul."

Moments later, Chronos stuck his head through the doorway. "If you're done feeling sorry for yourself, there's something you should see. Now."

Azrael lifted his head. "You found her?"

"Not exactly—"

He dropped his head back onto the pillow. "Then go away." He returned to studying the constellations.

"Don't make me drag you by your wings."

"Get. Out." He glared at Chronos, wondering why he couldn't take the hint.

Chronos looked over his shoulder. "I need some help."

The bedroom doors burst wide and Kol sauntered in. "You have any idea how pathetic you look?" He glanced at Chronos. "If I ever fall in love, promise you'll yank my shades off and stick a mirror in front of my face."

Azrael swung his feet off the bed and stood. "This is my home and I want to be alone in it. I don't care what you think, just get out."

With the strength only a Thresher could muster, Kol grabbed his arm, yanked him out of the bedroom and into the hall. "Move. The longer I'm here, the more likely I am to break something." He put a finger to a vase displayed in a niche by the doors and gave it a push.

Pulling out of Kol's grip, Azrael caught the vase and righted it. "I hate you."

Kol grinned. "I know."

Resigned, Azrael followed a chuckling Chronos out of the house and onto the front landing. The same ever-present twilight colored the surrounding fields. Nothing new. Certainly nothing worth being forced out of his home.

"What is so important you had to drag me out here?" Azrael glared at his brother.

Chronos simply pointed beyond the pearl paved drive.

Azrael followed the line of his finger. Beyond the glow of the pearls, coming out from the closest edge of the farthest field was a group of Shades, Vitus in the lead.

"My staff is back. I'm sure I would have noticed that when they entered the house." He pivoted on his heel to go inside.

"That's it?" Chronos asked.

"What did you expect me to do, sing the Hallelujah chorus? I appreciate that they're back, but it does little to assuage what I'm feeling." Facing into his empty house, he leaned heavily on the doorframe. He was exhausted and heartsick and done. "I just want to be left alone."

He slanted his eyes at Chronos, hoping he'd understand. But Chronos' attention was elsewhere. He peered toward the Shades, eyes darting from one to the other, and shaking his head slightly. "No, I meant was that all you see?"

Without looking, Azrael sighed and moved to close the door. "Yes, that's all I see."

Kol grabbed his arm and spun him around. "Look again. Look closer."

Azrael studied the Shades more intently. Vitus was still in the lead, beside him was the cook. Behind them was a Shade without the form and substance the Fates had given the rest of his staff. A glint of silver sparkled at the Shade's neck.

He shoved off the doorframe and stood at the edge of the landing.

"Sara." The word was a whispered prayer, a wish, a hope. It was everything left inside him. "Did they..." His breath hitched. "They found Sara."

He ran to meet them, grinding pearls beneath his heels, and reached Vitus in moments.

Up close, the glint of silver at the Shade's neck seemed little more than a dusting of moonlight. He glanced at his butler. "Is this Sara? Did you find her?"

Vitus nodded, smiled and reached for the Shade, bringing her ahead of him.

Azrael studied the nearly shapeless waft of mist and light. The face held no distinguishable features, the hair floated around her head like seaweed caught in a current.

"Sara?"

The Shade nodded, the slightest of smiles lifting her mouth. She raised a nebulous hand to caress his cheek, her touch a gentle breeze, and mouthed a word Azrael understood easily.

Home.

Chapter Twenty-five

"You owe me this much," Azrael said. "I reap souls for you without question, and you've given me nothing but misery in return."

"We gave you your staff." Atropos was unusually placid today. Her eyes hadn't met his once.

"And that's all I'm asking for. A form of more substance. Her features back. Just enough that she is the Sara I remember. So she may see herself in a mirror and know who she is."

Atropos shook her head, but Lachesis rested a hand on the old woman's shoulder. "Sister, Azrael has suffered much. Perhaps unfairly."

Atropos canted her head, a spark of anger in her eyes, but Lachesis didn't let her speak, continuing with a gentle smile for Azrael. "Let us talk a bit and we'll give you an answer."

With a hand around her waist, Lachesis helped Atropos inside the newly restored mansion. As soon as they disappeared, Azrael slumped against the balustrades.

Chronos nudged him. "I told you it would help if I came."

Azrael's gut was too twisted to answer, so he simply nodded.

The shadows lengthened by a hand span before the Fates returned. Hope sparked in his heart at Klotho's shy smile.

Hobbling forward, Atropos finally met his gaze. "You may ask nothing of us again."

"Understood." Anticipation crawled his skin like ants.

"Since you married the mortal, against our wishes I might add, we didn't feel she deserved the same status as your household staff."

Pain creased his heart. Chronos put a hand on his arm. "Stay strong, brother," he whispered.

Lachesis nudged Atropos gently. "Tell him the truth of it, or I will."

Atropos sighed. "After careful consideration of the mortal's thread, we've determined you were not the cause of her cancer. It was in her before you, and we think, the reason she could see you to begin with."

Azrael felt his jaw go south. "You mean you didn't even have a hand in her seeing me? After everything you led me to believe—" He started forward. Chronos' grip on his arm held him in place.

Atropos hobbled back a step. "Which is why we've decided to make her a Reaper of Mercy as well." She waved her cane, dismissing him. "We're through. Go home and explain to your wife why she has wings." She turned, headed for the door.

Lachesis shook her head and offered them a sympathetic smile. "You have two weeks to teach your bride everything she needs to know before we'll expect her to begin reaping souls." She winked. "Whatever those lessons entail."

* * *

"Where is she?" Azrael mounted the steps of his home two at time toward the door Vitus held open. He wanted to see her. Hold her. Touch her.

The butler pointed down the hall and in the direction of the bedrooms.

"Thank you." Azrael jetted past, racing to reach Sara. He burst through the doors of the room he'd created just for her. She stood in front of the cheval mirror, flexing her new wings. They were lighter than his, nearly white. She looked more like an angel than he ever had.

She turned, her face a bright beacon of joy, and ran to him. "Oh, Azrael, I didn't think they'd grant you anything, let alone this." Once in his arms, she glanced over her shoulder. "I have wings. Wings!"

"So you do." Wrapping her tight, he drank in her scent, her warmth, her sweetness. He kissed her repeatedly, covering her face until she laughed. He put a small space between them and sought her gaze. "Then you understand what they've done to you?"

She nodded. "I think so. They've made me a Reaper? Like you?"

"Yes. It wasn't what I asked for, but that's how the Fates are, forever doing what they think best. Are you okay with this?"

"It means we get to be together, right?"

"Yes. For always." He hoped she fully understood what eternity meant.

"Do I get a flying horse of my own? I think that would be so cool."

"I have no idea. We'll know if one shows up." He cupped her face in his hands. "This is forever, Sara. Just you and me. There's much you don't know about this place." He sighed. "You may wish things had ended differently."

"Like what don't I know?" She crossed her arms and narrowed her eyes.

"Like...there's no real daylight here. Only twilight and night."

"No daylight ever?"

"None." He knew he should have told her this sooner.

"Is that why there are mirrors everywhere? And that driveway of pearls?"

"Yes."

She uncrossed her arms and shrugged. "I'm okay with that. We can see the sun all we want when we go back to Vegas to celebrate our first anniversary. Now, back to the flying horse. I really think I should have one."

He grinned. He liked the way his wife thought. "I'll see what I can do."

"This is the most wonderful thing that's ever happened." She squealed and clapped her hands against his chest. Her wings fluttered. "I feel amazing! Like I've just won the lottery." She tossed her head, rippling her long brown newly wavy locks. "Not to mention I've never had better hair." She kissed him. "I love you, and this is better than what I'd hoped for. Maybe the Fates aren't as bad as you think."

"You'll meet them soon enough and you can decide for yourself, but before that happens, you have a lot to learn about being a Reaper. I've got so much to teach you. There's your visceral form to master, whatever that may be. Your—"

"I think you'll have plenty of time to teach me everything I need to know, don't you? Besides..." She trailed a finger down his chest. "I can think of a lot of other things I'd rather do first. Things we already know how to do very well."

"Sara, this is serious business. You've just become the First Lady of Death. You must learn to control your power if—"

"Ooo, the First Lady of Death. I like the way that sounds, but I'm going to stick with Queen of the Underworld. Much more impressive."

He rolled his eyes in amusement. His brothers were going to love that one.

"And don't worry too much about me learning to handle my power. I'm pretty sure I've got the basics down." She pinched her lips together, obviously trying not to laugh, but the mischievous sparkle in her eyes gave her away.

Heat flared between them. He looked down. Their clothes were gone. He bit his cheek to quell the surge of wicked joy coursing through him and did his best to keep a straight face. "So that's how you want to play it, huh?"

"Mmm-hmm." She nodded, leaned in and licked his bottom lip. "That's exactly how I want to play it."

Made in the USA
Charleston, SC
16 April 2014